THE
OLD SLAVE
AND THE
MASTIFF

THE
OLD SLAVE
AND THE
MASTIFF

With texts by Édouard Glissant
Translated from the French and Creole
by Linda Coverdale

PATRICK
CHAMOISEAU

Translator's Afterword: Édouard Glissant
and Patrick Chamoiseau

dialogue
books

DIALOGUE BOOKS

Originally published in France as *L'Esclave vieil homme
et le molosse* by Gallimard, Paris, 1997
First published in the United States in 2018 by The New Press, New York
First published in Great Britain in 2018 by Dialogue Books
This paperback published in 2019 by Dialogue Books

10 9 8 7 6 5 4 3 2 1

Copyright © Gallimard, 1997
English translation © Linda Coverdale, 2018

The moral right of the author has been asserted.

A CIP catalogue record for this book
is available from the British Library.

ISBN 978-0-349-70044-1

Typeset in Berling by M Rules
Printed and bound in Great Britain by
Clays Ltd, Elcograf S.p.A

Papers used by Dialogue Books are from well-managed forests
and other responsible sources.

Dialogue Books
An imprint of
Little, Brown Book Group
Carmelite House
50 Victoria Embankment
London EC4Y 0DZ

An Hachette UK Company
www.hachette.co.uk

www.littlebrown.co.uk

This work received support from the French Ministry of Foreign Affairs and the Cultural Services of the French Embassy in the United States through their publishing assistance program.

To Miguel Chamoiseau, who might
know where the Stone is.

P.C.

DOES THE WORLD
HAVE AN INTENTION

CONTENTS

TRANSLATOR'S NOTE

Histoire means both 'story' and 'history' in French, and through this story of a slave's flight into the unknown, Chamoiseau offers a cryptic history of the Caribbean, where many African peoples, stolen from their homelands and plunged into a Babel of tribal and European tongues, had to patch together what became Creole languages. Plantation owners used their own languages as a weapon of control over their traumatized slaves, who then turned that weapon against the oppressor: plantation storytellers said more in their homemade Creoles than their listening masters could ever understand, taking care, as Chamoiseau says in his *Creole Folktales*, to speak in a way 'that is opaque, devious – its significance broken up into a thousand sibylline fragments.' Which, if you think about it, is a fine definition of poetry.

Chamoiseau's novel offers loving and mischievous tribute to these Creole languages. In this novel are words and references from the history, culture, and natural world of Martinique, as well as both creolized and arcane French, because Chamoiseau is a free-range writer. 'My use of French,' he writes to his translators, 'is all-encompassing.' French readers are more familiar with this background material than are English speakers, however, so while the author does not want any Creole dimension of his work spoiled by the reductive ideal of 'transparency,' a translation must sometimes shine some light on these sibylline fragments for them to mean anything at all for the Anglophone audience. I have tried to make any explanatory material unobtrusive, while moving this text into English with the least possible distortion.

The majority of such Martinican Creole and creolized French words remain intact in the translation, either easily understood in context, or clarified by me with a descriptive word or two, or paired with an English meaning: '*djok*-strong,' for example. For more complicated words or a short phrase, the English will appear next to the italicized original text. Some words, as well as almost all the deeper background references (customs, places, etc.), are marked with an asterisk and explained in my endnotes, all listed by the number of the page on which they appear, in case any readers prefer to check batches of endnotes in advance.

Here is a look at the creolized French in the novel's opening sentence: 'In slavery times in the sugar isles, once there was an old black man, a *vieux-nègre*, without misbehaves or *gros-saut* orneriness or showy ways.' In Martinican Creole, *neg* means both 'man' and 'people.' It is *the default term for any Creole person of color*. It also means: a black man, any mixed-blood person, a servant, a friend, and has many compound forms, such as *neg-lakanpay*, a country fellow, and *gran-neg*, a pretentious fellow or uppity youngster. The Creole *vié-neg* is not necessarily derogatory – *vié* means 'old,' as well as 'ugly,' 'horrible,' 'shoddy,' even 'diabolical' – and here simply means an 'old man who is black.' *Gros-saut* looks like 'big-jump' in French, but the Creole *gwo-so* breaks down as follows: *gwo* means 'big' (among other things), and *so* can mean a bucket, a hard tumble, a waterfall, and the kicking of a harnessed horse. The expression *fè gwo so* refers to that last meaning, and its figurative sense is thus 'to kick, lash out at, be ornery.' So: the context suggests the interpretation.

One last remark about Chamoiseau's old man. In the original French title and novel, he is *l'esclave vieil homme*: 'the slave old man.' He also appears in the story as *le vieil homme esclave*: 'the old man slave.' The nuance is telling, and such labels continue to evolve as the tale progresses.

Chamoiseau introduces each section or 'cadence' of this novel with an *entre-dire*, an 'interchange' that opens connections among French literary texts. Here these links are short, evocative passages from *L'intention poétique* (*Poetic Intention*) and 'La folie Celat,' an unpublished text later revised in *Le monde incréé*, all works by Édouard Glissant, a fellow Martinican and a foundational figure of Caribbean literature. Chamoiseau thus opens a dialogue with Glissant about the nature of island identity in the West Indies. Glissant's powerful writings speak vitally to this story, and readers unfamiliar with them will find broad guidelines in the endnotes and my afterword.

Poetic epigraphs from *Touch*, an anonymous text, describe a meditative arc that moves ever closer and more clearly to the grand theme and climax of the novel.

Writing with both studied care and fond disrespect for words, Chamoiseau is not only free-range, but free-form. His syntax, lexicon, and punctuation (or lack thereof) can even be technically incorrect in French but must be respected – in this disrespect – by the English. In this novel, language not only tells the story; it *is* the story, an enactment of the subversive action it describes, and as the slave old man moves into a disorienting but exhilarating new dimension, Chamoiseau's parlance does too. As with poetry, the reader makes sense of the text, as an active audience for this storyteller. In the end, as Chamoiseau has said, *créolisation* is a matter of expressing a vision of the world, and my aim has been to make that vision accessible to the English-speaking reader in its moving and mysterious glory. Regarding the prickly counterpoint of sound and sense, and in homage to the *voice* of the Creole he champions, Chamoiseau sums up his instructions to his translators with triumphant glee: 'I sacrifice everything to the music of the words.'

THE
OLD SLAVE
AND THE
MASTIFF

1. MATTER

There is, before the cabin, an old man who knows nothing of 'poetry' and in whom the voice alone resists. Grizzled hair on his black head, he bears in the mêlée of lands, in the two histories, before-land and here-land, the pure and stubborn power of a root. He endures, he treads the fallow land that yields not. (His are the deeps, the possibilities of the voice!) I have seen his eyes, I have seen his wild lost eyes seeking the space of the world.

Immobile dream of bones,
of what was, is no more,
and yet persists in the foundation of an awakening.

Touch,
folio I

In slavery times in the sugar isles, once there was an old black man, a *vieux-nègre*, without misbehaves or *gros-saut* orneriness or showy ways. He was a lover of silence, taster of solitude. A mineral of motionless patiences. Inexhaustible bamboo. He was said to be rugged like a land in the South or the bark of a more-than-millennial tree. Even so, Word gives us to understand that he blazed up abruptly in a beautiful bonfire of life.

Stories of slavery do not interest us much. Literature rarely holds forth on this subject. However, here, *bitter lands of sugar*, we feel overwhelmed by this knot of memories that sours us with forgettings and shrieking specters. Whenever our speech wants to take shape, it turns toward remembrance, as if drawn to a wellspring of still-wavering waters for which we yearn with an unquenchable thirst. Thus did the story of that slave old man make its way to me. A history greatly furrowed by variant stories, in songs in the Creole tongue, wordplay in the French tongue. Only multiplying memories could follow such a tanglement. Here, careful with my words, I can proceed only in a light rhythm, floating on those other musics.

When this story gets under way, everyone knows that this slave old man will soon die. This conviction is based on no evidence at all. He is still vigorous and seems like an indestructible mineral, something *djok*-strong. His eyes are neither shining nor dull but dense, like certain backwaters struck by lightning. His speech keeps itself more elusive than echoes off a surfside cliff (and as inaccessible of meaning). He subjects his cabin to the maniacal housecleaning of the elderly, and his survival garden, scraped out beneath the trees, is a fine example of a fight against famine. So, nothing. Nothing suggests that his end is near except his incalculable age, which even the ancientest ledgers of the Plantation could not guarantee. The most wizened elders cannot remember the day of his birth, and no one still alive tasted the feasts at his baptism. Therefore, all are obscurely aware that his quarter hour upon this earth (that brief allotted span) has unraveled its last bit.

The Plantation lies in the north of the country, between the flank of a volcanic mountain and thick woods – woods of dark ravines bristling with the ruins of a forgotten time, woods of symphonic streams among the mosaics of rocks, woods of singing trees, peopled by opaline *diablesses** summoned in a riotous crowd by late-night storytelling into the audience-circle of fears. Sugarcane fields surround the Plantation, then go off to softly carpet the sea swell of humpbacked hills called mornes. Up there, they blur into the mists of the heights, glittering like molten metal. Down below, against the wall of woods, they end clumsily in a seething of muddy straw.

The Plantation possesses one hundred and sixty-seven slaves, women and youngsters included. Two mulatto *commandeurs* oversee the daily operations. The property belongs to a *Maître-béké* * whose family name boasts a nobil-iary particle. He clothes his absolute power in white linen, and a pith helmet gives him the allure of a conquistador fallen from a fold in time. He makes his inspections astride a chestnut Arabian horse given in exchange for rocky land by some shipwrecked Poles anxious to anchor their exile in a scrap of soil. The Master's wife and four children scrape by amid the mahogany redolence of the Great House, in the shadow of his unpredictable rages. His boys are pale and peevish; his daughter grows long honey-blond hair and flutters her lashes over staring eyes; his Lady amuses herself now and then with an ugly theatrical laugh that accents her mute melancholy. In his rare moments of leisure, and after Sunday vespers, the father fondles a formidable mastiff* used to hunt down foolhardy *foubins* who flee from servitude. No one has managed yet to foil the terrifying tracking of the animal. The Master doubtless adores it for that reason. The sudden sunshine of his smile breaks through only for this beast. And when, on his veranda, he saws away on a mother-of-pearl-inlaid mandolin, the mastiff sighs like an odalisque. The slaves in that area and those of the Plantation, as far away as they may be, give way to helpless gooseflesh at hearing that vile melody.

The Plantation is small, but each link among its memories vanishes into the ashes of time. The bite of the chains. The *rwasch* of the whip. The rending cries. Explosive deaths. Starvations. Murderous fatigues. Exiles. Deportations of different peoples forced to live together without the laws and moralities of the Old-world. All of that quickly muddles, for those gathered there, the rippling of recollections and the depth-sounding of dreams. In their flesh, their spirit, subsists only a *calalou*-gumbo of rotting remembrance and stagnant time, untouched by any clock.

Since the arrival of the colonists, this island has become a magma of earth fire water and winds stirred up by the hunger for spices. Many souls have melted away there. The Amerindians of the first times turned themselves into writhing vines of suffering that strangle the trees and stream over the cliffs, like the unappeased blood of their own genocide.* The slave ships of the second times have brought in black Africans fated to bondage in the cane fields. Only, it wasn't people the slavers began selling to the *béké* planters, but slow processions of undone flesh slathered with oil and vinegar.* These creatures seemed, not to emerge from the abyss, but to belong to it forevermore. The colonists alone manipulate the carnal masses of this heaving magma (baptizing, murdering, liberating, building, growing rich), but the planters seem more like fermenting matter than like living people, and their eyes, dictating the actions of slavery, undoubtedly no longer blink in any way validated by innocence, decency, pity. A fig for those miseries so often illustrated, let's put a name to this horror: the *grandiose in-humanity* that exploits human beings as an inert, indescribable density.

The Plantation is – after the fashion of everything in those days – disenchanted, without dreams, without any future one might imagine. The old slave has bleached out his life there. And, at the bottom of this slop, his existence has had no apparent rhyme or reason. Simply the hypocritical aping of obedience, the postures of servility, the cadence of plantings and cane cuttings, the *raide** marvel of the sugar born in the vats, the carting of sacks to the store ships in town. He has never been scolded for anything. He has never begged anything from anyone. He answers to a ridiculous name conferred by the Master. His own, the real one, grown useless, got lost without him ever feeling he'd forgotten it. His genealogy, his probable lineage of papa mama great-grandparents, is limited to the navel sunk in his belly, which *zieute*-eyeballs the world like an empty coconut hole, quite cold and with no age-old dreams. The slave old man is depthless like his navel.

He has known all the stages of the sugar industry. In his latter days – not because of failing strength but through vast experience – he deals with the sugar cooking, a delicate operation he performs without seeming to deploy any expertise. In the gleam of the boilers, his skin takes on the texture of the cast-iron buckets or rusty pipes, and at times even the coppery yellow of crystallizing sugar. His sweat dots him with the varnish of old windmill beams and gives off an odor of heated rock and mulling syrup. Sometimes, even, the Master's attentive gaze does not distinguish him from the mass of machines; they seem to keep going on their own, but the Master goes off again with the feeling that he is there – a feeling comforted by the correct aroma of the rising sugar and the oiled tempo of the turbines.

One never sees him dancing at *veillées*.* There slaves exorcise their own death through rhythm and dance, and tales, and fights. He has stayed in his corner, for years on end, sucking a pipe of *macouba* tobacco that sculpts his face in its severe glow. Certain dancers and *tambouyé* drummers reproach him for his apathy. Everyone spends their nights bringing their flesh to life, waking up their bones, and, above all, shoving their *bois-de-vie* – staffs-of-life – into the shady spots of the *négresses* drunk on *danse-calenda*.* They all thus project, into their feverish wombs, a future renaissance, like a different version of their own existence. But this crafty move aiming to survive death did not seem to interest our fellow.

The *commandeurs* take little notice of the slave old man, and have *pièce raison*, no reason at all, to do so. Bound to the Plantation like the air and the earth and the sugar, more ancient than the most ancient of ancient trees, and of no conceivable age, he has at all times insinuated himself into spaces of mindless motion. He does not serve (like certain *vieux-corps* old-timers, on other Plantations) as a memoir on the origins of the domain; has no opinion on the fertility of the different fields; announces neither weather forecasts nor harvest estimates from a simple sight of the first sprouts. The Master, questioning him, has indeed tried to make him into a voice of wisdom. Has even called him Papa as his father did, and his grandfather, and like his eldest son, who now does it too. But the antique slave wheedles no advantage from this, departs not a whit from correct servile behavior. Remains unalterable. No words, no promises. Compact and infinitely fluid in the gestures of labor that alone engross him in a faceless, locked-in life.

Even the slaves attempted to make a Papa out of him. A conveyor of Promised Land. An old-timey fount of wisdom and history. A guide, like the stake of manioc wood planted to pilot new shoots. A *Mentor*.* Often they questioned him about the Before-land,* the meaning and direction of the pathway ahead, the need to kill the Master, his offspring, his Lady, and burn the Great House. Rebels have sought his blessing right before their flight through the woods and their tracking by the deadly mastiff. But he never said anything or gave anything or offered the slightest hand to such magical expectations. His silence stirs up their fire: folks attribute powers and forces to him. They treat him as a *knower*, able to best the venom of the *Bêtes-longues** and wrest from plants the contradictory qualities of the remedy-for-all-ills and the perfect poison. He can, they swear, purge maladies, strip away the sorrows of life, postpone the grip of death itself, whose crony he seems to be. Hemmed in by their entreaties, he places his palms on mortal pains, or puts his lips to the knotted forehead of a dying man, or holds the stiffened claws of a sufferer heading off in agony to the Before-land. He kisses newborns, or touches the hams of someone seeking the nerve to run away. But he never does more. Even if certain miracles occur, even if he confers by chance through these gestures some strength, a courageous *contre-coeur*, a flicker of manly hope, his eyes still won't light up, or his skin give a shiver. Definitive, he takes on the opaque substance of that mass of men who are no longer men, who are not beasts, who are not, either, like that oceanic maw all around the country. They are a confusion of ravaged beings, indistinct in something formless.

Everybody winds up hating him. Then venerating him. Then hating him again. Then forgetting him. Then wondering how old he is. Then treating him the way one treats wretches from whom one no longer expects anything. With a somewhat puzzled respect, a neutral and slightly indifferent kindness. Thanks to this treatment, he, too, surely persuades himself that he has worn out his time. And although he gets used to this idea, it doesn't change his behavior one bit.

The only sign that this is all a mistake is that, one morning, on awakening, he does not answer the call. No one yelled out his name, of course, but his hand is missing in certain places where no problem usually occurs. A mule no one can calm down. Then a boiler that *macaye*, acts-up, when no poking around can find the cause. Then a sugar overheat that exhales toward the Great House the novel smell of singed caramel. Other annoying events leave everyone at a perplexing loss. Rats trotting in broad daylight all-round the cabins. *Bêtes-longues* flowing from the cane-brakes, their fangs spurting with anxiety toward the sky. *Mantou*-mangrove-crabs erupting from muddy dormancy to hang in clusters from the branches of orange trees. And green breadfruits falling unseasonably out of reason, denting the ground without cracking open. And *gangan*-mangrove-cuckoos, squawking boisterously over dead springs that suddenly start sobbing. Work in the fields – the end of the cane cutting – becomes more difficult. The *commandeurs*, having to call out more than usual, take a notion to use the whips. The slaves fear entering the fields where so many *Bêtes-longues* are going crazy. On the trails, they tread on sheets of red land crabs suffused with an odor of sulfur and mint. And more than one soul is scared to find on his tongue the *vieux-goût* nastiness of wormwood.

The Master has suspended his inspection tour: his Arabian horse rears with each step over invisible swarmings. Trying to understand what is happening, the Master must dismount and tramp through cane fields, then around the buildings of the Plantation. He goes, eyes wide and staring, without a word to say. His wickedness has so organized the world around him that the current derangement strands him in a highly indignant stupor. Nothing has changed but everything is slipping sideways: a kind of chemical decomposition, impalpable but major.

A trade-wind breeze has stirred up some dust. It robes the world in an anxious grayness accentuated by the sun's shackles. The Master proceeds, turns sharply, peers carefully around him, merely an attentive observer, barking no orders to anyone. He seeks the essential cause of this general malfunction, the pulsing seed of this intangible disaster, but finds nothing that might account for these bizarre little hitches.

So, he sits down on a front step at the cane-trash house. His horse, pawing the ground beside him, bends a nervous neck toward the ground. The Master looks now and then to the heights where his Great House stands out against the sky and sees the frightened forms of his wife, his children, and some house slaves. Huddled close, they peer out at a property apparently unchanged but as if suddenly set aflame at its core. The Master remains that way for hours and hours, meditating on this burden of bad luck. What has happened to those ritual protections planted at the four corners of his lands? Has the rooster's head sealed beneath the stair landing of his house lost its shielding powers? He is still closed in such calculations when a clairvoyant *négresse* advances to tell him, in the sunny flash of her teeth, 'It's that one who's escaped his body, *oui*.'

The slave old man – most docile among the docile – has gone marooning.*

The Master abruptly realizes that for a long time already, the mastiff has been howling, and that this howling, all by itself, *défolmante* – is dis-in-te-gra-ting – the substance of his world.

2. ALIVE

The fugitive – the African doomed to the injurious islands – did not recognize even the taste of night. This unknown night was less dense, more naked, it was unnerving. He heard the dogs far behind, but already the acacias had snatched him from the hunters' realm, and, man from vast lands, thus he entered another history, all unaware that there, times were beginning again for him.

Principle of the bones,
mineral and alive,
opaque yet organizing.

Touch,
folio II

The mastiff was a monster. It as well had voyaged on a ship for weeks in a kind of horror. It as well had experienced that void of a voyage via slave ship. The black flesh, crammed into the hold, enveloped that sail-winged hell with a halo the monster's rage perceived and the sharks pursued across the ocean. As had all those who came in to the islands, the mastiff had endured the constant rolling of the sea, its unfathomable echoes, its engulfment of time, its irreparable dismantling of intimate spaces, the slow drifting away of the memories it engendered. A sea that penetrated flesh to harry and thwart its soul, or decompose it, replacing it with the petty rhythm of nauseating survivals, small deaths, bitter routines, the martyrdom of carcasses that must cope with disorienting uncertainties. The mastiff had known periods in the open air as well, hoisted on deck early by a strangling chain and there, goaded on by the lash, the dog was forced like the black captives to go around in circles so as to limber up its muscles and inhale a bit of iodine on the high seas. And the wind itself, dazzling as an onrush of darkness, would put the finishing touches on the devastation committed by the sea in the depths of those nights in the 'tween decks. The dog would stagger along, limp like a jellyfish. Then be sent back into the dead angle of a stern gangway, that tomb (its cage): the after-hold.

The dog's gaze resembled that of the sailors. And worse: the wraiths who rose from the hold (weighed down less by their chains than by their shattered souls, and who sometimes threw themselves overboard into the sharks' jaws or suddenly, arching their bodies, swallowed their tongues, or even fell in wasted rage against the bayonet protecting a captain's throat) had that same gaze. Only the ship itself, through its rhythm of waves, the snapping majesty of its tall sails, seemed to live and to keep those captives alive. The mastiff was a monster because it had known that absolute collapse.

It came from who-knew-what Gehenna in Europe. No one knows the precise color of its coat, either. No doubt it changed *aléliron*: constantly and everywhere. The ship's cargo manifest recorded it as white with a black blaze between the eyes. The sailor who handed the dog its water and salted hide through the bars of the after-hold described a black coat with a white patch on the muzzle. On the Plantation, they saw it black, gleaming into a lunar blue, with a few white spots that maybe moved around. But (while it was demolishing their leg tendons) the slaves it had caught had sometimes seen it red, or blue-green, or perhaps possessed by the vibrant orange tints of a living heart of fire. As for the eyes, better not mention them.

The Master had bought the dog without any haggling and was probably the one who had brought it straight from Europe. He had set the animal beside him in the carriole. The two young male slaves, the little *négritte* girl, and the Provençal pottery from Aubagne purchased that day had all been packed into the mule cart driven by the slave old man. He was the one who escorted the Master to the big city where the slave markets were held when the ships came in. There were fewer such arrivals after the abolition* of the slave trade, but there had been a time when the Master had gone there often, even not necessarily to buy anything at all. He enjoyed the atmosphere of those torpid boats. Their crews (wild beasts) had known lands beyond those known, and behind the abattoirs sold melancholy objects and old portulan sea charts. Their shore leaves filled the taverns with shabby nonsense about ghost ships, women with seaweed hair, rash revolutions nullifying the blue blood of kings, or nameless peoples who pierced their lips with golden straws and drank bright blood in homage to the sun.

Sometimes, these ships came into port wanderingly drunk. Their cargo would then be discovered in irons, dried out by hunger and the fevers that strike one yellow. The 'tween decks and rigging were deserted. The orphaned sails were turning into great parched leaves and the lines coming untied enough to be called ropes for hanged men. The crew had foundered in the grip of a mystery. The casks of oil, salt meat, or potable water wriggled with the same worms, which seemed to await (or foretell) an end to time. Each belaying pin on deck gave birth to tiny flames that fainted straightaway in a musty whiff of *basilic*.* No one wanted to acquire the chained-together wrecks hauled out of the holds. Without even feeding them, the Governor chartered a military steamship to ferry them to some oubliette along the coast of Brazil.

It was, for the slave old man, a bewildering moment: watching men come ashore who looked so much like him. All poorly recovered from the most drawn-out of deaths. The oil disguising their sickly skins mingled with their sweat and the remains of miseries. Their screams, so familiar with extremes, had left the corners of their mouths forever foamed with garlicky crusts. They still bore some smells from the Before-land, some last rhythms, some languages already in despair. The slave old man felt they were incanted by those gods of whom he still retained illiterate traces. And the ship affected him as well. He no longer knew if he was born on the Plantation or had known that crossing in the hold, but each swaying of a slave ship in the calm waters of the outer harbor revived a primordial rocking within him. Crackings and snappings, muddy shadows, and liquid lights peopled the depths of his mind fuddled with slimy algae and marine *hautes-tailles*.*

After the Master, the slave old man was the first to see the mastiff. The slave old man and the mastiff looked at each other. The mastiff had barked *tout là-même*, right-on-the-spot. And even more than barked – it burst the bounds of utter slavering rage, its coat bristling every which way like a lion's mane. The Master had displayed his delight at this reaction, convinced that black flesh whetted the dog's appetite. He'd cajoled the animal with a hunk of fresh meat, a little special water collected during a thunderstorm, and the mastiff had so calmed down that it never again barked at anyone, not even the slave old man. Who, faced with its enigmatic fury, had remained as usual: more opaque and dense than heartwood of the *bois-bombe* charcoal tree burned seven times and the same again.

Those two saw each other every day from then on because the Master had put the animal in a vast kennel fenced in on all sides, between the Great House and the sugar-works buildings. Everyone passed by at some moment of the day or week. The monster was there, at this strategic knot, this inescapable crossroads. Lying full length on a quivering flank. Persecuted drowser, or bundle-of-nerves irritated within the confines of its pen.

The Master owned other, smaller, Creole dogs. Six or seven. They stood guard around the Great House. They barked whenever *nègres*, chicken hawks, mongooses or *Bêtes-longues* went by. They were barbarous of bite, for they were kept tied up the livelong day. When they ran as a pack, they amused themselves by chomping on one of the house slaves, or by 'molishing the leg of an old slave woman beached near the boilers, where the dogs lapped up the many-colored crusts of molasses. For which the Master never scolded them. The slaves hated these dogs in a way that can no longer be imagined. Sneered at them, too. They tossed them repellent poisons that could stiffen them at one go and prevent their flesh from rotting in the lime pits; heavy rains always exhumed their damned mummies off in some corner of the property. But their numbers were never exhausted: intent on stocking his surroundings with these canine alarms, the Master was constantly buying more off an elegant mulatto who had lost all sense of shame.

The day the mastiff arrived at the Plantation, the Creole dogs had yowled from afar. As the carriole had drawn closer, they'd plunged into a fury unheard of for their kind. When the carriole entered the circle drive, the mastiff leaped to the ground. The dogs shut up, *flap*, seized suddenly by an ominous *quiet there* they would only rarely abandon in future: for some *nègre* gone astray toward the Great House, or some specially sinister cyclone, or some earthquake revealed in advance to their hysterical senses.

The slaves feared the dogs, but they were appalled by the mastiff. Its massive body was like a slab of sulfur, its muscles bulged like lava bubbles; the pitiless face, unbaptized; the gaze, unseeing. The most chilling thing was its silence. No barking. No grunting, yet no calm or serenity. Merely, above its bated breath, that scrutinizing stare, honed-filed-sharpened-trenchant, with which it followed the living souls that went by its fence. Whenever a Creole dog got loose and came skulking around its cage, the mastiff did not even budge. The prowler would lie down belly up, whimpering, offering submission simply to a flick of this monster's ears.

The Master fed it in a strange and, above all, secret way. Palpitating meat. Bones with flaming marrow. Bloody fleshy things that he kneaded himself in a Carib warrior's skull. In which, some said, he crushed together wasps, hot peppers, hummingbird heads, snake fats, bone-powders from rabid men, the manes of crazy *chabines*,* the bones of mother-big barracudas, and the brains of mama ballyhoo needlefish. The mastiff devoured it all more from dark determination than from appetite. In a few months, it regained that incredible strength the ship had worn away. Even-more-compact flesh. Muscles supple as cables when the Master took the dog running on a rippling rope for hours, atop his chestnut going at a steady gallop just to keep up with the beast. And the horse, mightily out of sorts at having that around its hooves, lost a little more of its joie de vivre.

Folks wondered what this monster could be for. They soon had their answer. There was, as happened almost every month, a young *nègre* convinced he was wilier than his predecessors and who was hit out of the blue by *la décharge*. I am going to tell you about the *décharge*. The old slaves knew about this: it was a bad sort of impulse vomited up from a forgotten spot, a fundamental fever, a blood clot, a *désursaut pas-bon*: a not-good jump-up, a shivering summons that jolted you *raide* off the tracks. You went around being taken to pieces by an impetuous inner presence. Your voice took on a different sound. Your gait grew gently grotesque. A religious flutter set your cheeks and eyelids trembling. And your eyes bore the customary fiery marks of awakened dragons.

The *décharge* would take you at any moment. It was invoked to explain those desperate, hopeless attacks on *commandeurs*. Those slave hands that grabbed their throats *flap!* That cutlass *rachée*-slash launched despite the pistol that would shoot down these madmen who never had a chance. The *décharge* would send you hurtling above all in frantic flight into the forest. Then the Master would pursue you astride his Arabian steed with his pack of yipping little dogs. He always caught up with the runaways, and rare were those who managed to dissolve into the humid shade of the very tall trees. The Master said as much. He never announced, 'So-and-so escaped.' He would say, 'So-and-so evaporated into the woods,' satisfied to know they'd fallen victims to the zombies he claimed infested the forbidden high-forest.

So, this slave youth had his *décharge*. And, instead of cutting a *commandeur*'s throat, he went off, just like that yes, *en plein mitan du jour*, at high noon, abandoning his patch of land with an endless cry and beelining for the nearest woods. *Marooning!* . . . The *commandeurs* chased after him for an hour but could not catch the smoke from his heels. They then trumpeted on a conch shell to alert the Master, who came running. The Master took stock of the situation, squinted up at the hills, listened to the muteness of the tall trees. Then he smiled (unexpectedly), but no one had time for surprise: the mastiff, off by the sugar works, had begun to growl. Not bark, but growl something astringent and acid and irresolvably evil, which revealed to everyone how the monster would be used.

The Master rode to the fenced-in kennel and fetched the animal at the end of its thick rope. The mastiff had stopped growling. It was now alert, staring up at the hills as if following some invisible movement with its muzzle. It neither strained at its rope nor tried to quicken its pace. In the runaway slave's cabin, the Master had it smell a few rags from the pallet. Then, together, they headed for the silent Great Woods, leafy with rooted mists and lost dreams. The slaves followed the chilling team with their eyes. The Master, the horse, the mastiff: an accord old as eternity seemed to unite them. To mix-combine them.

They advanced in a single movement, with the same deadly resolve. Nothing could deflect them, united in their mission.

The Master loosed the mastiff at the first *raziés*-undergrowth. The animal plunged in without barking, without growling. One heard only the stunning energy of its paws hammering the forest floor and the Master followed this calmly, his blunderbuss slung at his shoulder. Afterward? No time for an afterward. *Redévirer* : they swiftly retraced their steps, with the black youth – savaged – dragged at the end of the rope, the attentive mastiff weighty at his side. What the animal's teeth had done was seen close-up. Which the Master had wanted everyone to notice before he applied his pepper sauce.* The mastiff had mangled his victim better than the wickedest of whips and the most barbarous board-of-nails. The young slave walked forevermore like an old man, stuttering, with empty eyes.

The mastiff had returned to his kennel without further ado, placid and watchful once more. The slave old man saw him that way every day but never stopped in front of him as did the unthinking little children of the slaves. Because grown-ups, even the most scatterbrained, avoided having the dog 'take' their scent. With that in its nostrils, it could sculpt you in its dreams, taste in anticipation the splendors of your blood, and above all capture you with ease if you bolted in a *décharge*. So folks avoided the place, and the children, as the track-downs continued, abandoned the

idea of the dog as entertainment. But nobody noticed that
he, the old man slave, passed all along the kennel fence. Et-
cetera times a day, without glancing sidelong at the mastiff.
Without looking it up-and-down. Sometimes he even went
by as the Master was opening the cage to bring it flesh and
bloody tidbits, and smile at it, pet it. Nobody noticed either
that, in the presence of this slave old-fellow, the mastiff
became even more watchful, a tad more on the qui vive, a
stitch more lying-in-wait, in a flawless *raidi*-stillness of its
iron frame. In Creole folks cry that: *véyatif o fandan. Vigilant
to the uttermost.*

The mastiff expressed the cruelty of the Master and
that plantation. It was pathologically alive. When the old
man slave went by the fence, it followed him with eyes of
fire. Now and then the old-fellow shot back a glance, something gliding and lusterless. And their eyes would meet for
seven nths of a second. The confrontation went on this way
for months. The mastiff brought back six or seven *nègres
marrons* from the forest. Tore the throat out of a black-
black-*Congo* woman possessed by a *décharge*. In time, he
seemed even more deplorable. And although the *décharges*
remained a constant (attacks *sans manman,** some suicides or
volcanic lunacies), fewer and fewer slaves were seen fleeing
toward the woods. The mastiff mounted a ferocious guard
over these captive souls. So you know everyone was dumbfounded to see that the old man had defied the dog anyway.

But how on earth had that been possible, with him so old

and close to death? I will, without fear of lies and truths, tell you everything I know about this. But it's not much.

The old man has never joined in at the slaves' celebrations or the *veillée* storytelling, when the *paroleurs*-talkers tell how to defeat the mastiff. He does not dance, does not speak, does not react to the cattle-bell summons of the drums. He seems inert but manages to decipher undecodable things. His presence reinforces the drumming of the *tambouyés*. It brings them mysterious speed and *balan*-élan that fill them with joy. And he slakes his thirst there. In his company the dancers – without even realizing it – discover unsuspected muscular resources. The songs as well surround him, as they do the others. But the old singers who shiver with automatic memories – those lovely purveyors of nameless words – cultivate in secret the happiness of having him there listening to them. All – but not in so many words – suspect he is a shining sun of memories and try to bask in his light. And he, undaunted, accepts this gift. He plays the drums without playing them. He joins in the dancing while remaining stock-still. He stocks his soul with scattered, reconstructed, lopsided things, which weave him a shimmering memory. Often, at night, this memory crushes him with insomnia. The *Papa-conteur* of the Plantation was a rather insignificant fellow (an African *nègre-guinée* with small eyes, a board-thin body, and a slightly hunched back). He transformed himself when he began to speak (wide eyes, burly body, beautiful

bearing). He breathed in the life around him to invigorate
his words. And thus he awakened life. He spun speech –
parolait – and launched laughter. And the laughter loosened
and swelled everyone's chest. Their hatreds, desires, the
lost cries and the silences expressed themselves through his
mouth. When the Master disembarked all sudden-like, a
commandeur at his side, to seat himself benevolently on the
outskirts of the circle with a *galoon* of rum as a treat, and
began to answer the *Krik-Kraks*,* the *Papa-conteur* did not
shift his speech. His selfsame utterance pursued its course,
circulating things that few beings could appraise. Yet the
old man slave takes sustenance from that. He untangles the
obscure parlance of the tale, knows hatred, desire, and fear,
experiences a thousand stories come from Africa, a thousand narratives brought back from forgotten Amerindians,
from the Master himself and, of course, from the mastiff.

The *Papa-conteur*'s words carry him off to strange bor-
ders. They give him flesh in the flesh of others, memories
that belong to all of them and quicken them all with a
wordless throbbing. The Master cannot see it, but there
are so many shattering and bewildering presences in the
old man that he must (like the other slaves) increase the
inertia of his skin, the gentleness of his gestures, the drawl
of his heartbeat, the bluntness of his face. He must *go on*
with these forces inside him, maladjusted beyond measure,
which do not explain anything to him about himself, or
about so vast a life in this most cramped of deaths.

At night, cast sleepless ashore inside himself, he confronts incomprehensible chasms, stifling densities, tempos combined according to muddled laws that hurtle into uncertainty. Worlds are dying in his depths, and these agonies give him no respite, nothing but more entanglement that only dancing, the drums, the words of the Storyteller (as they go on fathomless) can soothe. That's why the old man seems so cataleptic at those *véillées*, savoring the balm spread on that *blesse*-wound seeking its own sense. The Word of the Storyteller does not come to him in speech: it carries along too many tongues, too many cries, too many silences. It is like an inborn song felt above his belly. With a few impossibles stuck in his throat, without participating in the appeals of the Storyteller, he *launches his presence* at him like a silent hand. He offers him his spirit, some specters of remembrance, and prophetic pains that glisten in every scrap of his flesh. His flesh: that virulence preserved unmoving from which the Storyteller always knows how to drink deep.

The *décharge* had scourged the old man many a time. No one had ever known. Some felt the thing only once in their lives, yet he had endured it almost every day. Day after day, and most often when it was slackening off among the others. The first time, it had set him writhing on the dirt floor of his cabin in the middle of the night, with the irrepressible longing to *hurler-anmoué* (scream-for-help), *dé-courir* and run counterclockwise to undo bad luck, *saisir-déraidir* in a seize-up-go-limp confusion, or plain strangle something. He'd calmed down by eating earth and scraping his forehead against a wall, which had released a shivering heat that gentled his mind. The other times were during the day, in the fields, in the sugar-sack carts, at the port, on the roads when he was the coachman, then in the grease of the boiler shed where his life was wearing itself out. And every time, his body became a burning stone, an immense *ouélélé*-uproar resistant to *décantation* spell-breakings. He had felt like dancing, *bouler du tambour* – rolling with the drums, braying those incomprehensible sounds that were hacking up his head, but each time he had held back, knotting his gestures and actions and emotions like vines around a body gone berserk. That's how he became as placid as a backwater marsh. Stiller than a *chapeau-d'eau*, a water lily. He must live self-contained to control his fits of *décharges*. No movements. No useless words. No raised eyebrows or voices. Nothing but the impeccable mastery of motion, mind and gesture compressed to a murmur, the blood's dance reduced to a minimum, an eruption noted solely in the immobility of the most terrible deaths or the most stolid substances. It is his only way of living and being – as no one knows – catastrophically alive.

And he rediscovers in the mastiff the catastrophe inhabiting him. A gimlet-eyed fury that lashes out from afar. This inner chaos carries along things that don't belong to him. He seems possessed by presences other than his own, but his self, his very being, he cannot find anywhere: no spine of memory, no helpful pattern, no ridge beam from a time when he was a distinct entity. Nothing but this boiling up of violences, disgusts, desires, impossibles – this magma triumphant on the Plantation and making him what he is to his core. And the mastiff is like that as well. But in the animal's impressive ferocity, this catastrophe has pulled itself together, becoming a blind faith that can master the dire trouble born on the ship.

The old man slave does not remember the ship, but in a way he is still down in its hold. His head has become home to that vast misery. He has the taste of the sea on his lips. Even in the light of day he hears the dramatic snouts of sharks against the hull. He also remembers the sails, the crosstrees, the lines – as if he had been one of the crew, all mixed up with visions of the Before-land, and even more than visions: women, beings, things, beauties, uglinesses that quiver within him, are him, and mingle with the open chaos. The mastiff is like that, but it commands a mass of instincts that delude the dog into seeing sense there, a meaning now tied to the taste of the bloody flesh the Master feeds the beast as the meaning of existence. The dog is the Master's rudderless soul. It is the slave's suffering double.

Our old fellow goes back and forth around the dog for those mysterious reasons. Confronted by inner anarchy, he finds himself drifting toward the animal. He has no need to look at it: the mastiff lives inside him. His look of the living dead has never fooled the dog. No doubt the monster perceives in him a passel of possibilities. It sees itself bound to this old man slave who gives off no vibration at all, nothing but the brute density of unplumbable matter, crammed with damps and slit-eyed suns. The mastiff's cruel vigilance perceives this confusion. On each approach, the slave old man feels the trouble capsize him, the chaos submerge him. Right by the fence, he does battle with the forces within him. They awaken, fly together like magnets, lay waste to him even more fiercely. *Charges and décharges!*

He had seen the beast race off after the runaways. Had seen it return. He had seen the dread it inspired in the slaves' evening vigils and how its mere presence stripped their dances of energy. He had seen how the Storyteller had begun assigning insane attributes to the animal. This mastiff, he said, was the watchdog of hell and the dead. He gave it the body of a furry bird, a feathered horse, a one-horned buffalo, a carnivorous flower, or a mute leprous-toad *crapauladre*-man. Masoned from wounded moon and the mother-water that forms crystals, its flesh was the guardian of precious gates. He said defeating it would lead to joys as yet unnamed. He described the dog on subterranean voyages, flanked by shadow-spitting suns. Sometimes, he appointed it the jailer of a swarm of glimmerings fluid as a virgin's tears. He described it decorated with palms beside unimaginable tombs among budding new births. He told of it eating some unalive-things cut up for it by old men in accordance with the movements of the stars. He said it could stare into the glassy eyes of the deceased and there awaken nine times three times seven souls. He saw it guiding pregnant women onto the bridges of destiny and leading them to term. He always placed the dog at turning points, stream-boundaries, passages and chasms, shortcuts and alleyways. He saw it draped in leopard skins, stretched out above its master, offering its auguries to those who swallowed its flesh. He watched it call up words that only the prophets strove to name. He saw it clinging to the solemn shoulders of mystic initiates and gratifying their liturgies with a cruel wisdom. He saw it gobbled by ghouls, ogres, grotesque chimeras until it changed itself into a quite pure and most enviable clarity. The old man slave listened to all these tales without hearing; understood without understanding. He was attuned only to the distant murmur they knotted inside him.

From the moment the animal arrives, the *décharges* become terrifying. He who has believed himself the master of this chaos now sees himself go under. From then on he fears the *décharges*. Fears they will carry him away into pathetic gestures against the triggers of the *commandeurs* or the Master's flintlock musket. Fears no longer being himself and suddenly appearing before everyone's eyes as a *nègre marronneur* who never did dare. Try as he may to become pure matter when drawing near the dog, that beast awakens his turmoil in extremes that leave him stupefied. That's doubtless why he had the feeling of death: the substance of his soul was struggling, chaos was seeking its cry, and the cry its word, and the word its voice. So he decides to go away, not to maroon, but to *go*.

Therefore, he prepares nothing. Neither salt, nor oil, nor water, nor big *bi* chunk of boiled cabbage. No ruminations, no grim glance toward the woods. He is even more motionless, placid to the last bit of him. His actions around the machines grow more fluid as the chaos stiffens inside him. This irrepressible force – on that day – lightning-strikes him against a boiler. His skin touches the hot sheet of metal. Sizzles. He thinks he's losing his head under a welter of pains suddenly loosed at him from everywhere. But his practiced mastery regains control. His skin comes out of it intact. His vision does become troubled, and in this trouble he can see landscapes that blur his eyes. He sees quicksilver roosters celebrating evangelical nights and moulting into snakes before they dissolve.

He knows he is ready.

He does not know what for.

This time, when he approaches the fence, the mastiff rises. The old man slave stops. For the first time in so many years, he looks at the monster. Which slowly comes closer. Staring. Studying. Ears on edge. Muzzle slightly frothed. Standing still, facing the old man slave standing even stiller looking back at it. The slave old man gestures toward the dog in a way he himself does not understand, an imperceptible movement no one sees but which the mastiff follows with its icy eyes.

That night, the slave old man feels not a *décharge* but a combustion. His body becomes a prey to convulsions. A great heat knots his limbs. Every object in his cabin sweats blood all ablaze, and the polished earth underfoot takes fire as well. He sees himself surrounded by gleaming lights drawing tiny orbs in the air. He fights these nightmares. He is heard (who hears him?) moaning. Then groaning harshly as if feverish, but no one worries because suffering no longer moves anybody. Before dawn – when a healing glint prepares to rise from the earth to prophesy an innocent sun – the slave old man straightens up. He puts on his coarse linen livery. He settles his old *chapeau-bakoua** straight upon his skull. He grips his staff and leaves, tranquil, his step vibrant with a holy energy. He passes among the cabins, crosses the cane fields, where the *Bêtes-à-feu* – fireflies – watch him go by. When he reaches the first trees, the mastiff springs to attention. Although already far away, the old man slave feels a shiver along his back. He turns around toward that Plantation where he has worn out his life; he looks at the distant buildings, the sugar-works chimney with its leaping flames, so familiar; he hears one last time the sound of the now-widowed machines. The shiver slips away at his nape. Then, the slave old man plunges into the tall trees. The ancient howl of the mastiff begins to undo the domain, provoking the eleventy-thousand strange little hitches already described, and faced with which the science of slavery gave way.

3. WATERS

The cask burst; Marie Celat* saw the seafloor there. No growth from clays or black earths, only the basalt *mornes*, sown with green-mantled cannonballs, and those traces that memory chewed down to the quick: the mark shredded into the bark, the *Bête-longue*'s vertebrae and the gunpowder to cram into the *nègre marron*. Through the cask Marie Celat saw a horizon of sky blossoming out of the forest. Then she climbed to the summit of this *Morne* that nobody has managed to descend. The one who does battle with the beast awaited her.

Reflections of the bones,
sole images sans images
of the gestations and agonies.

Touch,
folio III

The old man ran. He quickly lost his hat, his staff. He ran. Ran without haste. A steady pace that took him surefooted through the back-of-beyond-*zayonn* undergrowth. He sent his body across dead stumps, laid low the kneeling branches with his heels, hurtled down reclusive ravines devoted to pure silences. Around him, everything shivered shapeless, vulva dark, carnal opacity, odors of weary eternity and famished life. The forest interior was still in the grip of a millenary night. Like a cocoon of aspirating spittle. Another world. Another reality. The old man could have run with his eyes closed: nothing could orient him. Sometimes he bumped into unseen little branches, his toes, ankles, face – whipped! He had to run behind his bent forearm to protect his open gaze. Then, as he went on, the trees drew closer together in the thickest of pacts. The boughs fastened themselves to the roots. The *raziés*-underbrush gave lavishly of its irritating prickles. The Great Woods loomed. His pace slowed. At times he had to crawl. The enveloping vegetation stuck to him, sucking, elastic. With bleeding elbows, step by step, he made his way. It went up. It went down. It *monta-descendre*: up-and-downed. Sometimes, the ground disappeared. He tumbled then into sheets of cold water that gurgled with emotion.

The old man felt close to the sky. The stars diffused a blissful radiance etching the forms of the ferns. But the darkness – so intense – sent that pallor to him in a starry dust: it dissolved all forms. Often he headed down again, he had the impression of descending endlessly, of reaching even the *fondoc*-fundament of the earth. There he thought to find the vomiting of lava or the fires said to flame from the *foufoune*-pudenda of *femmes-zombis*. The torn *rachées* of his heart throbbed within him, stirring liquid, glowing embers that shattered his body to rejoin the sky. Such incandescence summoned up wild earthy fumes in his bones. Leaves, roots, trunks, took on the odor of ashes graced with those of green corn and newborn buds. Water, invisible, showered in drops from certain large leaves; at other times, it became a sweat that greased his skin until he seemed covered with scales. Unsettled by an incontrollable energy, he was neither hot nor cold. He did not feel the *raide* licking of water or those thorns prying at his fingernails, or even those sharp branches that in trying to disembowel him made a lovely mess of his livery.

Nothing seemed able to extinguish his energy. He proceeded like a ship at the mercy of a liquid womb. From going up and then down, and feeling up high after coming down, he no longer even knew where the sky was, where the earth lay palpitating, which side was his left, where to go to the right. This was no longer the earlier absence of landmarks but a profound disorientation. He advanced with the impression of standing still. At times he felt he was backtracking even while convinced he was heading for the heart of the Great Woods.

In the beginning, he had been scared shitless. He expected to suddenly see the monsters feared by the folktales: the impish *Ti-sapoti*,* the dog-head women, the fireball *soucougnans*,* the flayed-flying-women perfumed with phosphorus, the unbaptized misery of *coquemares*,* and the persecuted zombie persecutors. But he saw nothing of all that. He saw nothing at all. Except this tragic blackness. This slapping, lashing vegetation. This energy living inside him as a stranger. The more he imagined the monsters, the bigger his eyes grew, the wider his mind opened, and the more the darkness maneuvered around him. His skin grew sensitive to the acrid breath of winds bruised beneath the leaves, to the velvety touch of the dewdrops that clung to him, delighted to be visited after century-times of solitude.

His skin became porous, then it became powdery, then it must have gone away because he thought he came apart in an effervescence amid which only his bones supported him. In time, the Great Woods wrapped-him-up-tight. Forced him to be still. Stillness was, there, a plunge into the abyss and an elevation. It taught him the nausea of mummies and of people who are brought back to life, the confused panic of those walled up alive, and the exquisite bitterness of the martyr's coma. Abruptly, this hold on him let go as if at the entrance to a cradling clearing. Then he ran with all his might, jumping at random over imaginary tree trunks, swerving aside at random, lying down at random, leaping at random, advancing according to the laws of a dance that allowed him, all unknowing, to avoid a thousand obstacles before a green hand grabbed him once again. It took him a while to realize this: a magnetic prescience let him be a bole, a moss, a branch, a spring, a tree. He flowed within their traceries. He no longer felt their shocks, or else passed through them like a cloud of pollen. He felt as if he were a shadow, then a breath, then a fire, then opaque flesh that restored to him – brutal – the world's horde of sensations.

Soon, he was not conscious of anything. His body no longer perceived itself. Persevering in his flight, he pinched his limbs, touched a wound, brought a lick of fresh blood to his lips and was reassured to find it tasty. That was not enough to put him back together. He experienced the distress of ruins that had once been sumptuous cathedrals.

The Master claimed that the runaways he had not managed to catch had dissolved into the Great Woods. This fugitive felt he had become water within the water of the patient leaves. He had no fear whatsoever, *pièce pensée* – not a jot of thought: nothing, save the motionless onrush of that dark mass that lived inside him and surrounded him. So then he strove to go faster, jump high, run *raide*, fly far, meld all this together through speed. It seemed to have no effect. He thought he was dying, losing his struggle against life's miseries, and expected to emerge from the cold glue of a nightmare, but patting his face gave that the lie: he was indeed *bien éveillé, bien réveillé* – wide awake, well awakened. Then he muttered the word *éveil, éveil léveil*: awakening, awakening th'awakening, opening his eyes wide without fear of seeing them burst by a branch. *Éveil léveil*. He saw nothing. Felt nothing. Only this motionless aspirating movement. *Éveil léveil* he feared he was dead, buried by mistake in a nail barrel,* and some old reflexes returned. He was forced to listen to himself in unknown zones, to isolate the sound of his heart, more powerful than ever. He perceived the giddy whirl of his blood that he had slowed down all his life. He experienced, as if torn, the sensation of every bit of his body, every unknown organ, every forgotten function. He apprehended the circulating sun that united and drove them. His run had propelled his flesh to its ultimate limit and his formerly separate organs, reacting en masse, passing beyond all distress, kept on going, leaving him panting with innocence in a hazy awareness of himself he had never known before.

Plenitude. His perception encompassed the darkness around him. He recovered the feeling of displacing himself, changing position; he avoided the trees with calm authority, and moved through the undergrowth with ease and a fine air about him. He chose no direction, sought nothing in the hopeless darkness. Fearing a return to his starting point, he conjured up for himself an awl of light emerging inside him and toward which he swiftly *donna-descendre*, began to descend. This fixed point gave him the illusion of orientation and its immediately beneficial reassurance.

He apprehended his aroundings differently. The desolate darkness revealed to him the texture of humus, the tangled ages, the regal waters, the pensive strength of tree trunks, the verve of the sap hidden in this vegetation. All this was enhanced by a profusion reflecting great energy. This élan sustained him from that moment on.

Suddenly, the light was different. Painful. Daybreak had arrived. Gluey luminescence came down the tall trees. A foggy dawn suffused their trunks and drowned the underwood with milty mist. He saw a tortuous – blood-ied – vision – but shut his eyes and ran more vigorously, overcoming obstacles like a rush of water. No time to drink from the springs, where his heels sank in deep. He had no desire to drink there: water seemed to impregnate him. Immanent, it slaked his thirst from within. Now and then he half opened his eyes and found himself lashed by ever-more intense light. His eyelids burned him; he kept them shut tight. He thus avoided discovering those great unknown trees in any way other than through the obscure alliance now familiar from those initial hours. He tore off a strip of his livery to make a blindfold. His race toward the luminous point spiraling within him continued like that. Inside. All out.

The point vanished when he heard a brutal growling pitched high.

Far away.

Not a yowling, but a jaggedy howl.

The mastiff was hunting him.

Fini bat . . . Battle's over! he thought.

He sped up but was dismayed at losing his point of light. So, then, he bent his spirit toward the earth. He listened, all ears, to the pretend silence of the soil, teeming with hay mushrooms, the burrowing of roots, the dense panting *uh-huhs* of boulders, the limpid light of scattered streams like copper-bright sighs. He listened some more, desperate, then finally heard. *Thumps.* Muffled thumps. Bitunk. Bitunk. Bitunk. The pounding of the monster's paws pursuing him. They almost matched the rhythm of his heart. Then he accelerated to make those rhythms one, so that he might use this sound sent to run him down as a guide for keeping his distance. *Fini bat . . .*, he thought again, mulling things over.

4. LUNAR

A single disordered sweep of lianas, strangler figs, tiring bamboos, brown mahoganies, which drag the past along as far as the Pont de l'Alma. The acomas of the heights still sow along the slope, to meet the sea-foams and burn-beaten lands, the scrawny acomas down below, their children, which neither astonish nor strike fear. Here rises not one tree's cry like a solitary mourner, but look: the surge of those vehement masses swells, where you must clear a way along the Trace.*

Mirror brightness of the bones,
organic night total
of every promise of living.

Touch,
folio IV

The Master has never seen this. He releases the howling mastiff. At the end of the thick rope, he follows it along the skirt of the tall trees. And there, among the twisted roots, the lace of ferns, the monster does not know in which direction to dash. *The old man* a pris disparaître: *has done disappear.* The Master himself, expert in the tracks left by runaways, searches for a tiny rumple in the thousand-year-old tropical silva. Nothing. The slave old man appears not to have passed this way. Or slipped by that way. The mastiff and the Master walk along the edge of the tall trees (their almost human murmurings brush lightly past like old folks' breath) until break of day. Mechanical, attentive, the mastiff advances: sniffs, fine-tunes its ears, stretches its neck and quivers its spine. It seems to be taking its time before bounding away. It finally finds the track (a sour rustling in the innocence of the virgin *raziés*) but does not hurtle off as usual. With the wary step of a *molocoye*-tortoise, it pulls the Master beneath the greenish shadows; he must soon dismount and follow on foot. The chestnut horse stays behind alone, leafy, covered with shade and vines, terrorized by murmurs none of its instincts seem to recognize.

The mastiff becomes a reptile in the venerable wilderness. As for the Master, weighed down by his musketoons, he has to blaze a path with a cutlass. Although the blade opens an imperious breach for him, he must brush away the netting of the bird-eating tarantulas. The long curtains of leaves give way beneath the blade and spring back, splashing him with sap. Soon he must release the mastiff, reel in the rope, wind it around his waist. The animal ventures alone beneath the dark vault. The Master strains his ears toward its velvet tread. Then, he hears it run. The Master tries to follow it closely, convinced the slave is ensnared in a knot of prickles, but then must abandon the fantasy: the mastiff is penetrating the interior at a long-distance pace. The trail carries the dog far, *au fondoc dépassé*: beyond the back-of-beyond. The Master speeds up some more, then tires. He keeps in his ear the hammering of those paws, reverberating off the tall trees like the echoes in conch shells. He advances on alone, connected to the percussions of the racing animal. *Oala*: from that moment on, the Master feels uneasy, his *bon-ange** upset. It dawns on him that the trees are truly murmuring. Not at him, but these murmurings worry him, so deeply is he registering them in the very clearing of his skull. Without admitting it to himself or truly understanding this, the Master believes he can no longer go back. He believes himself obliged to advance forever into this everlasting half-light. The Master feels alone.

The old man rediscovers a primordial darkness. Revealed by the blindfold, it is not comparable to the darkness at the beginning of his flight. This night neither envelopes the trees nor flows from the sky. He knows it is released inside him as he runs. He senses its growing *épaissi*, its *thickeningness*, like a patterning of the *balan*-rhythm of his running. It seems to allow him to exist a little closer to the center of his being. His skin is skimming up the promise of the coming sun. Infinite variations solicit his dermis: the earthy aura of the tall trees; the increasing keenness of a shaft of light; the oceanic armpit of a ravine; the mummified silence where ferns exhale the odor of eternal death and stubborn life. For the moment, he has no sensation of going up or down. Suspended within himself, he travels through a sensory topography that molds itself to his body. His eyes whirl, crazy beneath their lids and the cloth blindfold. He pays strict attention now to the noise of the animal's paws; then, as he races on, he loses contact. Or rather, he registers it differently, among the cadences rushing from his heels. The trees seem to change. Doubtless more ancient. Seriously silent. Sometimes disapproving. The old man feels himself penetrating into the cavern of ages. No one seems ever to have trod upon that place. The impression of entering a sanctuary becomes intoxicating; an untold authority asserts itself over the darkness within which (and with which) he runs. He understands the sensation that so overwhelms him: *A-a, sé kouri an fondoc syèl . . . Oh, it's running right in the sky,* he thinks, weeping. And he opens his arms in a cross, each finger an avid root, sentient leaves.

His mind warps. Slowly. He glimpses forms: troubled, troubling, all threatening. Impossible to identify. They come from nothingness. They flow toward him. There is this. There is that. They are legion, of all sorts without kinds or categories. And-then there are looks without eyelids, scattered in clouds where amniotic showers are brewing. And-then maws gaping open like gates without doors. And-then left hands netted in the grip of a language. And-then upraised-arms and musician lips. There are nine hairy waves of terrors. And-then suffering fleshes he feels he might know. He thinks he is gone-crazy and tries to tear off his blindfold. But the prospect of dawn's dazzlement restrains him, as does the idea of opening his eyes upon those unknown trees. He quickens his pace, provoking an onslaught of hallucinations. Clacking-paks. Rolled-rollings.

Moans stuffed under wicker baskets and agonies that shatter mirrors. Bright vitalities and the languors of gentle counting-rhymes. Flounderings of hatred. Rains of bloodlettings and seed. Broken shells, religious shames, how many women's emotions, enormous milky breasts, murky not-very-manly desires, how many delicious sins and infectious innocences. How many intimate collapses, including even the worst heartbreak-*coeurs-cassés*. All this frightens him, without being unfamiliar.

Suddenly, a somber *ouélélé*-hubbub; it's also a sound in the Creole tongue; it's also the drifting of a lot of languages; he recognizes a voice; the swing of a wake-wailing; warbling registers of unclear words from which he plucks their exemplary energy; it's sharply, at times brightly black, directly rooted in unbelievable valor. It brays a vital commandment inside him. A call of life. A call to life. He feels in fine fettle. The visions multiply; he clings to this green vigor that seems like a voice to him. It is human human human. Virile and maternal. It appears to spring from a close atmosphere of silence and death. *Elle trouble l'existant*: it stirs up his being and existence. He believes that this voice arises from the storytellers known during his enslavement: these men, arising one after another, indefatigable, forging a way of speaking that no one understands but which baptizes everyone. He no longer remembers their appearance, they were that insignificant. But irises of their language stem up now from the most extinguished part of him. The mastiff on his heels is showing him his own unknowns.

The hallucinations surge back through this force, which is sovereign like a primal voice in some biblical land. The hallucinations make images. He sees a lady with black skin, an arresting gaze, wearing silky foam that opens a corolla of petals about her body; she transports souls in an oxcart, rope-hauled over a single shoulder; her steps affright the dust and she limps on the goat's hooves deforming her ankles. He sees, clustered on three acacias, sad-eyed children who grow enormous enough to crush their perches. He sees awkward horses on the horror of three-hooves.* He sees lively stoppin'-coffins kicking up the dickens at the four-corners of thirteen roads. He sees devils in silk-cotton trees* in commerce with three lovely livid *chabines* decked out in curl papers or seaweed braids. He sees Agiferrant,* that colonial settler of a moon, bearer of a mango tree shaped like a double cross. He sees a *Kakouin*-sorcerer who opens for him the route to routs. He sees zombies with tree heads, or else no arms or legs, or else with big tits. He sees some *bons-anges* who have lost their way. He sees some guardians of treasure* whose nostrils send clay bits flying. He sees the *Ti-cochons-sianes** devoid of any family in the pig race. He sees blocks of blood that scatter into shrieks. He sees the dream* about pigeon peas, and the one about the tooth, and the dream about midnight, and the one about the bread-loaf heel. He sees the *Pamoisés** with their crooked thumbs. He sees the spirits one can hire to do dubious things. He sees some *Dorlis** counting up the grains in a calabash of white sand. He sees *la Bête à Man Ibè.** He sees phosphorescent froth, then the forgotten shore, familiar, laden with a musty odor of savanna and tall, disillusioned trees in countless numbers. He notices a yesteryear of childhood in some very bygone songs; and some liturgies; and some initiations celebrated with beer and sesame oil in lonely languages. He sees the grottoes of knowledge where the great masks sleep, and the *nez-bec* beak-nose dancing the seven sequences of a sixty-year cycle. He sees the lumbering dances of seed-time, the showers of rice and the hands crowded with green boughs. He sees the living masks in the pact of plumes, and the spark that reveals their song. He sees the guardians of poison and maleficent forces, O kindly quaffers. He sees woven textures of memories where clay carves births amid the raffia grass. He sees in thin strips of cloth the infinite interlacings where the wind knows how to sing. He sees the vertigo of uneven swerves in the art of forgotten embroideresses, the thronging gaps of lights, the couplings of fulls and empties in the labyrinthic nuanced colors of ochres and saffron. He sees the meanders, the netting and the signs leading wanderings in the velvety raffia. He sees the bird that offered cotton, the fish that gave the spindle, and the spider that revealed weaving. He perceives the drums that go back in time. There are women's voices nursing twins on shards of pottery. He sees the calabash-spoon, and the millet pestles, and sacred cups borne on a donkey's back. He sees the androgynous couple on the cradle of the world. He sees sovereign shapes, sculpted in the great-dark of myths, set in a total time, patinated with drippings from sacrifices. He sees himself blown through by sea blasts, makes himself *gibier-volant*, a bird, then finds himself on coral beds, buffeted by shark jaws, weighed down by chains, and drifting around the *en-bas* – the deep-down – of the most somber of seas. He sees himself as bone powder transforming into seaweed and rusty chain links. He sees skulls sheltering translucid fish. He sees the dawn of an old sun and the outcries of precious lands. He sees himself in chips of stars so shattered they melt down to a tenuous gleam. He falls. As is. Laid low.

His awakening is a startlement. A fear. The old man feels he fell like that for plenty hours. The mastiff has doubtless caught up and is standing over him. He balls himself up, rolls into a root, thrashing like a castaway in the foam of drownings. No growling. No wild animal odor. He calms his body. His heart fills the universe with its extreme beating. His breath pumps steam like a forge. It sears his throat. He stays like that for an unknowable time, less exhausted in body than devastated by that experience. Packed tight within him, those visions get ready to pounce again. He doesn't dare move.

Nothing stirs thereabouts. The trees chew a cud of eternity. The too-fermented air sediments a thin sticky skin onto him. He hears a whistling. Then another. Then still another, worn away by the distance. It petrifies him. *The Unnameable. The Unnameable.* He no longer knows if the deadly fangs are moving toward him, or if they spring from his fevered mind. He waits. Forcing himself to calm down. Seeking that mortuary calm perfectly polished over so many years. He feels at home in his body. His muscles twitch from tumultuous energy. Alive, as if intoxicated. A last bit of courage comes to him. He begins to listen. And it is then – exact – that the fear surges back. Not-even-imaginable disruptive force. *He no longer hears the animal's paws.* Nothing. Except the omniscient prayer of the tall trees, the breathing of the brushwood, the quaking of the insects. The germinations bound to the immutable silence. The monster has stopped running. He is no doubt already there. In position. Ready to *racher*-rip out his throat. The old man who had been a slave feels lost once again. *Cacarelle*-shitting. Wilting heart. But he does not move. He stays still as mangrove-water. He is listening, straining to the utmost. Listening *comme cela s'écrit*, to the letter: impeccably. Nothing. The animal tracking does not echo anywhere. The old man feels a relief that makes no sense: perhaps the monster has given up.

This relief runs through his body with a trembling like a sudden *embellie*-blossoming of sunshine. But another feeling grips him. That of the beast, straining terrible toward him. He feels it. It is there. It's coming yes. To launch itself on him. Biting. Jaws. Cracking of bones. Bleedings. Slaverings and swallowings. *Huh*. He imagines the cruel approach through the ageless tropical forest. *Huh*. He thinks he sees the cocoa-brown eyes. The *sans-manman* fangs. *Fer.** Fer.* The old man who had been a slave begins to call out, *héler*. And even to *rhéler-anmoué*, shout-for-help. In a reflex of lost faith, of blood under pressure, of a *bon-ange* in eclipse, he removes the blindfold. And this reflex has the astonishing perfection of a warrior's flourish.

5. SOLAR

After all the years we have been crossing, without seeing our own footprints, here at last comes the time to trace back the names.* They have gone to ground on the heights; haul them into the daylight of today, yet without naming them. The mystery of the name is a valiant spur to dig deep in reclamation! When you trace swiftly from the source, and well before encountering your carnivals and your car-gluts of nowadays, you run raide into this lump of lava, which chills.

Fertile cement of the bones,
Secret socle of creations
and re-creations.

Touch,
folio V

The light was wounding. *Un fer.* The shadow inhabiting him spun around on the axis of a coming-apart. Panic-stricken. The old man found himself in the leaf litter. His pupils were just glowing embers. They were searing his skull; he attempted to tear them out. The shadow within him tried to protect itself. It charged like a seventh wave* entering a tumultuous outer harbor, then swept back in a *macayage*-puddle-muddle. He felt spellbound by desire; *coco*-cock turgescent, balls loaded, eleventy dazzling *décharges*, cum from seminated seminating suns, lunar spangles of semen. A shaming *la-honte* took hold: hug his nudity, bury old fears, cover up this anguish. Light was leading flocks from one pasture to another in him. It was scattering innocences.

Great guilelessness was crumbling under lucidities like lesions. Densities were disuniting; a gaggle of times he felt multiplied and reduced. The rest is impossible to describe in this tongue; let ancient sounds and languages be brought to me, an array of vocal qualities, tonal sheaves and effervescent liaisons: I am a construction site for new geneses. Yes, light was leading migrations in him.

Taking advantage of this light that was demolishing his equilibria, sooty flashes tried to overwhelm him. They seemed to arrive from everywhere: furrows of earths, *zinzole*-zigzags of talkings, *siwawa*-abundances of peoples, big bouquets of persons. For the first time since he had confronted it, the roiling magma seemed to gain the advantage. Yet light was in him, openly pillaging, chilling. Unknown architectures reared up trembling, then strewed themselves around in thundering downfalls. A meshing of lights-and-darks hemmed in his mind. Feelings of giddiness. The old man who had been a slave managed to get onto his knees, and-then to hoist himself quaking, back flat against a trunk, and-then to totter, and-then to attempt returning to his footrace. He was running under the urgency of agony. Every step triggered *l'avalasse*-cloudbursts of brightenings and smoke-gray flows. But he was advancing. He was managing to advance. He believed that speed would re-establish the lost equilibrium. Light poked fire through his now transparent eyelids: he had lost them, and his pupils were exposed to the unbearable glare. He ran on, or he tried to, in any case he had, in a *balan*-élan through the Great Woods, the blind sensation of advancing. But the earth gave way. A *manman*-big hole. Deep. The old man who had been a slave was engulfed in a trice.

He had fallen into one of those old wellsprings that nourish the deep-woods. Drowning. Icy-icy water. He encountered once again the nightmares of the slave-ship holds. The abysses. The windless sea. The salt. The waves. Gape-jawed sharks. The water. The water. He was going to drown at the bottom of a spring. He sensed its intense vitality. It came from afar, companion of chalky densities and clayey pits, carrying along a way-back dream of sulfur and phosphorus. It remembered marine fossils, stellar alluvia. It had seen tabernacles of gypsum and iridescent caverns carved in basalt. It shared complicities with beaches and volcanoes, the singsongs of the sky murmured by the rains, the poetry of the isles in the advent of a grandiose era. Subsidences had deflected it, and erratic faults had shunted it (for twenty-two thousand years) into underground evasions. A few blind roots had sucked its substance and been nourished. Thus had the spring kept itself at the surface, nibbling the earth without gushing from the soil, digesting it slowly, enough to call forth a trouble of a marsh. Like an eye of water, an absorbent maw beneath the undulation of blissful ferns. The tall trees suckled there; they defied the sun with an insolent verdancy that the thorns of the dry season could never beat down. The old man who had been a slave told himself he would die there, at the *fondoc* of that fountainhead like many another *nègre marron* no doubt, swallowed by the woods and never glimpsed again, gaunt, near a chicken coop. He smiled: dying in the living entrails of a spring older than he was. Hmm. It tasted like storms, all savory from the alcohol of silty rivers. It seemed irradiated by coal and sky, by volatile essences and extinct sediments, anise-flavored roots and flowers with the scent of angelica. He felt imbued with purity. He drank of this splendor that was already flooding his lungs: he desired it so much. The sun that had blinded him had lost nothing of its glare as jagged as a manioc grater. But, at the bottom of the spring, the glare had gone black. Intense like certain women. And the spring itself, as he was drowning, was turning black. It was invading him black. An obscure clarity seized him as he gulped to find himself some air. He understood what death was: this dizziness of course, this endless sinking, but also this spurt of primitive matter where one will come apart. He tried to shout a *help!* of sorrow and pain. Oxygen tragedy. He tried to coo with pleasure, so happy to see the end of his suffering. He was dying. *Finir-battre. Battle over.* White earth. Warm mud. The tormenting light was now in alliance with the shadows that had possessed him, and he experienced the last feeling of falling. To such a point that words fail me. The beyond-words and the beyond-reach-of-writing of song and of crying out, there where I mourn (so poor) my impossible desire. The old man who had been a slave was leaving swept away by the ultimate mystery. Vanquished.

A hiccup. Where all light and all shadow dissolve, there is an *envoyer-monter*: *Go!* An elemental will-to-live. The old man who had been a slave began to struggle. His chest became a blacksmith's bellows. His feet fumbled for a convulsive foothold on the sightless roots that crisscrossed the spring. He found something to push off against. He shot out of the hole to inhale air. He fell back and sank far into a sludge of mercury. He rebounded, grabbed a gulp of air. Then another. And another. With each surfacing, he filled himself with a bit more desire to live. He leapt, body arced, catapulted. Shrieking to shreds.

His hand closed around a limp vine. He used it to free himself from the marshy suction. He crawled over the flimsy layer of leaf litter. Saved. Ethereal contentment flooded through him until he caught sight of the crabs. He had fallen into a mystery of tangled crabs. Frights of legs and carapaces. Ancient *mantous poilus*: big hairy wine-purple mangrove crabs. Swarmings of huge lurid red claws. In fact everything was red. Light had taken the upper hand in scarlet voltes that filled him with strength. He kept his eyelids *serrées-clouées*: nailed-tight-shut. He crept as far as he could from the lunatic crabs and the mortuary spring that was singing a dawn. A *manman*-root (rolled up about itself like an autistic goddess) became his refuge. There, he began to laugh, with the alcoholic laughter of those torn from tombs after old misunderstandings. Body saved. He laughed like this. *Comme pipiri chantant*: like the gray kingbird singing *pipiri!* at daybreak. Roasting coffee at first light. The smell of a good coal stove. Trembling water on opening petals. The sacred sweating on a barrel of aged rum. He laughed like that, and the energy of his laughter pounded his body. He was surprised to feel nothing of the tumult that had possessed him. Calming down, his heart had followed the curves of a tranquil breeze, flowing-river-strong, yet peaceful. His muscles, unstiffened, had paused in the soft comfort of shelter. An evangelical feeling never known before. So, he had the desire, the courage, to open his eyes, or rather, to move his eyelids. He still saw red. He saw troubled. He saw doubled. Light was strong but no longer as violent. It came from the outside, doubtless from the inside, shining upon him sweetly. The things around him were formless, moving, as if seen through very clear water. I opened my eyes wide to see better, and the world was born without any veil of modesty. A vegetal whole in an imperious evening dew. I . . . The leaves were many, green in infinite ways, as well as ochre, yellow, maroon, crinkled, dazzling, indulging themselves in sacred disorder. I . . . The vines sought out the ground to mix themselves up some more, try rooting, sprouting buds. I could lift up my eyes and see these trees that had appeared so terrifying to me in their great-robes of the night. I could gaze on them at last.

They were all immense. Each one nurtured the intangible in a mystery. They harvested light high, high up, and smuggled it to their feet as phantasmal contraband. Their branches sealed alliances of shadows and glowing openings. The vault of vegetation, braced against the earth, dispatched its trunks straight and wild toward the sustenance of the sky. Living trees, dead feet, green twigs, barren branches, parasitic plant hair, buds and rotting spots, seeds and broken blossoms, earthly night solar light – bound themselves together in one momentum. Plant life and death went on with this same ardor, in complementary but undifferentiated cycles. So then I, who had envied their impassive postures, I recognized them, I tried to name them, create them, re-create them. Here are the Acajous, armored in grayish bark, whose powder has often closed my wounds; here are their woody flowers where parrots peck at the garlic taste of their flesh. Here are the Rose Laurels, long nervous foliage, hirsute, whitish, so stimulating in teas; I'd used it to soothe my eczema. Here are the Courbarils – the West Indian locusts – with deep red heartwood whose miracle is revealed in the hubs of varnish distilleries. Oh, the Guaiacums, lignum-vitaes, more *raide* than rocks, soul of musky resin so good for my gout. *Mahoganisti-feuilles*, *Mahoganis-gwan-feuilles*, Small- and Great-leaved Mahoganies, yes it's you. Ho, yellow-flower Acomas, filtering the bitter breath that is eternity. Here are the redwood Carapates, clothed in the rugged black of which carpenters dream. Here are the *Filaos*, casuarinas discouraging to the ax, and the *Pieds-fromagers*, silk-cotton trees that rustle with *danses-zombis* and *la-prière*-blackbirds. Here are *Mahots-cochon*, and the *Pied-bois-marbri* snakewood tree, nurses of love, here are the Mauricifs, the dog cherries that tanners destroy, and the gloomy Sandbox trees casting shadows without leaves and whose seedpods explode. Here are the Balata bully-trees, and the immense Gum trees destined for *drivée*, ocean drifting; here are the Calabash-trees and the *Bois-flots* – balsa 'float-wood' – and the Bamboo clumps that take seventy years to ruminate a flower. ... They were all there, *Bois-rivières*, *Pains-d'épices*, *Géni-pas*, and if I did not see them, I could feel them coming up. Here are the Breadfruit trees planted by the Maroons, and the Avocado trees that mark their trails; here are the Acacias bearers of knowledge; there are the three Ebony trees* that anchor the axes of a strange saga. There they are, trees that the light clothes in secrets, or those that wrap themselves in a halo of *fait-noir*: darkness. All came out of the earth with the same force, as from a staved-in belly. I wanted to wallow in this earth giving rise to so many strengths. My need for these strengths made the trees beauties. And this beauty allied both the earth and the sky, and the night and the day. I covered myself with humus, then volcanic-ash tuff brought up beneath my scrabbling fingers. My body was discovering the appetite of roots, the gluttonous solitude of earthworms. My hands excavated clutches of black soil I rubbed on my body. A swarming escorted me:

snails, wood lice, and hawkmoth caterpillars, ants and milli-
pedes. . . . I was eating earth. It dissolved warm on my tongue
with an aroma of caverns and salt. The earth endowed me
with a feeling of puissance well beyond life and death. And
the earth initiated me into constancies I recognized as august
and everlasting.

I was seated. I shook my head to tear myself from the
hypnosis of the tall trees. Crouching, I listened better to
the fabulous silence. The sounds of the monster had not
returned. But it was coming toward me with all speed. I had
this intuition. If I did not move, it too would plunge into the
wellspring marsh. I had the idea of waiting there like that,
so it would stay the course and drown itself in the thousand-
year-old trap. I grabbed a dead branch, good for cracking
its skull. Then, I listened again. A fracture in the silence.
Its steps. Yes, I heard its steps. Impossible to know if they
were near or far. The trees scattered the impacts. Sepulchral
echoes that chilled my heart. At the same time, I realized
the crabs had rejoined me. The *mantous* were plaguing my
toes with their *gros-mordant* pincers. The red crabs wanted
to bury me in a blood-red pus disgorged by the leaf mold.
I swept away their front lines; this was like pushing back
water. With scratching legs, embittered claws, they came on
to replenish the devastated horde. I decided to move away
from the spring, reduced to hoping that the mastiff would
tumble in anyway. I was about to *prendre-courir*, take to my
heels, when – hoo! – I set eyes on the Unnameable.

The Unnameable was there, in the shadows, coiled on a fern at a level with my neck. Already tense, poised to attack in a *whoosh!* of scales. Hissing. Fangs bared. I was frozen, I mean stricken-blue-petrified. Time unrolled like a dropped spool of thread. I had the approaching threat of the mastiff, and jaws without a name poised to bite. I was between two deaths. I had, all my life, feared the slithering Unnameable. Some folks had quested of me the laying-on of a palm over Nameless bites. I had that way saved lives with a hand moist with fear, its only virtue the scald-chill of relentless primal fright: *la-peur*. Dark. Powerful. Sacred. In spite of the so-many years they spend deep in the fields, in the back corners of the sugar works, beneath the distillery casks, no Nameless had ever attacked me, no more than they ever struck at the smooth foreheads of stones. But here, this one was preparing to kill me. I sensed the unwholesome aura of its alarm. It stretched out toward my awakened flesh. My fear amplified its terror. Its venom had gathered at the base of its fangs, its crimson glands at the ready. I had gone cold-stiff: that had saved me. Now my blood was panicking again. Sweat varnished my brow. Terror was welding us together in a silent *vrac*-jumble. Our identical emanations were finding an equilibrium. This probably protected me. I had to stay like that. *Pas bouger, mon nègre*: stock-still, my man. *Pas foubin, mon bougre*: no fooling around, you bugger. No letting your heart fumble its fear. No letting the oncoming monster rip a shiver from me. Stay-here, with this Unnameable swifter and stronger than you are. If it injects me with venom, even spurts it over my damaged skin, I'll be done for. *Pas bouger.* Behind, the monster drawing near sent me a severe desire to run away: *Courir. Pas bouger. Courir. Pas bouger.* I did not know what to do. I thought I saw my death oh so clearly. Saw it even amid this tearing apart.

The monster had snatched up the trail at the edge of the Great Woods. An enigmatic odor, changing as it gained access to the knotted heart of the jungle. Thin at first like sighs of dry wood, it had opened into unbelievable perfumes. The monster had detected cemetery-mustiness, coming-undone flesh, disinterred sweats. It had no trouble following this odorous crisis thick as a rope and smelling so much like flesh both dead and alive that the monster had felt its speed increase.

Then the trail had changed again. It had mingled with stale vegetal aromas like a lace of liquor with endless variations. The mastiff had sensed fears from more than twenty thousand years. Genetic torments. Boiling bubbles of terror. This multiplied its impact on the ground tenfold. The trail had morphed into the astringency of wormwood, then almond, then camphor, which had asserted itself over the rain-forest fug. The trail soon had little left that was human. The mastiff's nostrils caught intrusions of pumice stone and battered basalt. For a moment it had thought itself pursuing an *aigle-malfini* – a broad-winged hawk – because of a whiff of fluorined rain. Then had thought itself hunting a phantom ship haunting Brittany* that tormented a master wrecker dreaming of boarding her. The mastiff had thought it was tracking the rank wolf of the great snows, or the ear-shredding mountain bear. It had thought of the Norman black ram for which one heated up a thirteenth silver bullet in a casket of mandragora. It had picked up on the musk of those weasels that rout gypsy caravans. Or that of the badgers pursued by master-scholars eager to mush their brains into anti-epileptic medicines. Up had come miasmas from cat bones* disinterred at night for their ability to turn everything invisible. At times, the monster had thought it was crossing those cornfields where each ripe kernel bore the image of a virgin and above which storms would melt away. It had had the feeling of running toward a sea where jellyfish swamped corals with their viscous suicides. Only the imperial continuity of the trail had allowed the monster never to go astray: the track varied infinitely without breaking and the dog had learned that was the thing, that was what it had to hunt, even when this hunt was like sticking its muzzle into the wake of a dusk and a dancing dawn. The monster stayed right on track. Its eyes (if that's what they were) never blinked.

The Unnameable petrified me and I petrified it. I had reached an innermost depth of despair. Dying there like that from a foul blow! The shadow I had repressed arose before me. The Unnameable is neither male nor female. The Unnameable has no beginning and the Unnameable has no end. The Unnameable appears to bear its double reflected in a sky scrap and earthly mirrors, and it can swallow itself and be born again at the same time. She has witnessed the birth of the most ancient gods, and he inhabits them all. The sun follows the curve of its flanks and the night nests in its very slithering. She is of water, he is of clay, and she is a drinker of rainbows. Medicine of life, medicine of death, the Unnameable is: sum of all fertilities and all sterilities. I had seen the deaths its bite would engender, those bodies swollen by a carbonaceous chemistry, those faces destroyed by massive suffocation. No tree grew on those graves, but the grass was delicate there and sensitive to the winds; it quivered with more divinations than the shells of seven-year-old conchs, and more than one gravedigger had had to toss in lime slices and pure coconut water. These remembrances buffeted my mind. Each of those images delivered its load of ambiguities into my fresh new vision.

My becalmed mind still swept along sea swells of former turmoils; they had the slackness of failed memories. I found once more in some corner of my soul the quietude that had flowed through me when I emerged from the hole. That appeasement was offered me. I settled in there again. All fear faded from my body. I was deep and dark and clear as the spring where I'd thought to die. I became a slip of cool breeze over savanna sand. An electric energy harboring the little-bird lament of the tall trees. I even believed my skin would change color like that of anole lizards. I was surprised by my transformations in front of the atrocious Nameless. It was coming to terms with me, and its dread was dissolving in the *embellie* of my emanations. I felt the pouches of its venom drain and its grip on the fern stalk relax. A conceited strength filled me; I felt, as the faster of us, like seizing her by the neck and crushing the vertebrae in my fist. I felt, as the faster of us, like sending him flying with a slap. I could do that. But I simply pulled away in a smooth move. She vanished on the spot. I feared he might abruptly reappear around my feet. I rolled over and over et-cetera of times. Then, I returned to my race, sending flying the shivering of crabs that had completely covered me. It was time, for the monster was nigh.

I took care, during my run, to baffle its sense of smell. I rubbed up against cinnamon bark. I smeared myself with the *fourmis-santi* stink ants that populate the *liane douce* – a wild potato vine – as well as big termite mounds, living on dead roots. I used vetiver leaves, *manicou*-possum nests, warm muds that smelled mysterious. While crying I'm sure, I handled the three leaves of *l'injonction-diablesse*, which convey invisibility. I knotted signs of escape to limp branches. Hand flung over my shoulder, I waved off any blinding spells. In fact, all leaves were good for me; I was hoping to dissolve into this forestine soul. Now I heard the animal's run in a different way. It had never slowed its *balan*, had never known fatigue. Its rhythm remained intact like a mechanical thing. I sensed in it a fury more ferocious than at the start. Doubtless because the dog had drawn closer to me. The impacts no longer resounded in a somber way; they crossed the leaf litter with precision. I who believed in nothing, I felt faith in everything: in these trees with tresses of melancholy vines, in these pale orchids on immodest roots, in these keeping-quiet birds nesting bracketed in low tree-forks, in these furtive presences that quickened the shadows. I invoked protection like a little lost child. I must have cried a long time, the run flinging my tears onto ancient dews. I mourned the misfortune of this dog that would destroy me, but I wept as well over this rediscovered life intoxicating my legs, this old heart burning the energy of a thousand years of living every second. I mourned this freshness discovered in my flesh, this magic in my eyes that enchanted the world, this mouth where tastes exploded, the sensitivity in my hands and the rest of my body. I had appetite and I was already dead. And I wept for all of that, without sadness or suffering, with all the less restraint – as I saw it – because crying was living and dying at the same time.

I saw clearly, but was advancing more slowly. Was it fatigue or the accumulation of obstacles? Detouring around tree trunks. Shoving aside bushes. Breaking the moorings of the lianas and the jackstraws of dead branches. My wounds were beyond counting. Clawed. *Griji*-grazed. Skinned.

Froixé-bruised. Swollen. *Zié boy*, half-blind eye. *Blesses*, hidden-hurts. I was covered in bright blood and scabs. I saw clearly and that clarity encumbered me. I rather missed my initial blind run. But this light had come to me to confront the monster. It was the wish and the will of life. Running, the mastiff was more alive and lively than I. Its hunger for killing, a good deal stiffer than my longing to live. It galloped, I felt, in the obscure grace that had allowed me to penetrate the *zayon*-wilderness better than a spectral *Dorlis. Ne plus courir, me battre. Not to run anymore, to fight.* Fight it. This resolve dismayed me. Excited me as well – truly unexpected.

So then I stopped, battered in my breathing. I seized a dead branch. Long. Heavy. Sharpened from a break. I had it well in hand. Ho, surprise the animal. I was hoping that the odors I had loaded on would cloud its tracking, that it would not know I was coming back in its direction. *C'est revenais que je revenais*: I was coming back with a vengeance. I was running the other way to meet it. My run became light-footed. It became coconut oil and silk-cotton fluff. I was not thinking about anything. An unusual plenitude bore me along. The decision to fight reintroduced certainties and hopes. It honed to the verge of madness my desire to survive. The race backward exalted this desire into a rage to conquer. Not a hatred, not a resentment, only a will-to-destroy what was threatening me. Loads of times I had, on buoyant *bois-flot* rafts, faced high waves to deliver

barrels or casks of sugar to merchants' ships. Heading into
the waves, negotiating them *exact*, using their opposing
unleashed energies to head up and across. An ancient
intoxication found again there, intact in the depths of those
Great Woods. My *boutou*-bludgeon in hand, I'd wound up
a hunter. Back to me came attack cries on bright savannas.
Many bled-out elephants and wild beasts roaring. Tracking
crocodiles in exhausted mires. Dances for the courage of the
brave. A *blogodo*-hullabaloo of peoples and very angry gods.
A dementia of four million years illuminated by towering
flames. I was going back toward the monster. I no longer
saw any of the earlier impediments. I felt myself a warrior.

I stopped *flap*. It was there. It was approaching, carried
along by its momentum. It must have been running like that
for heaps of hours, tied to the threads of my odor. I set my
back against a trunk, got a firm grip on my club. The inhaled
air had lost all oxygen. My eyes were now red and my body
was in poisoned-she-cat convulsions. My arms had gone
rigid. I felt rage and sainted fright. Only one blow would
be possible. Fracture its face. Bash in the jaw so it breaks a
vertebra. A single vertebra snapped; my body, saved. Strike
with decision, not with strength but as a block of energy and
with unerring aim. I made ready to do so; I imagined myself
doing this; I assured myself I could do this. I took the time
to breathe deep, slowing the anxiety of my lungs begging for
air. I took the time to get used to my all-worked-up muscles.
Air entered me like a sea breeze, a motherly nursery rhyme

nestled in a rocking chair, a banjo strum at the pink of a dawning day. I exhaled – at length and slowly – my confusions and fears. That made my vigilance giddy. I was ready. *Bandé*-aroused to the uttermost. And relaxed as well.

The mastiff was approaching. Appalling, the power of its paws. My doubts came rolling back like a widespread tide. The paws' impacts were clearer, like twacks on a drum. They punched in the earth. And their rapidity was beyond comprehension. That speed would make it invisible. I would not see even a wisp of its smoke. I feared lacking time to launch my blow. *Fesser pile: thrash fast*. Strike true. I adjusted to the dog's gallop, gauged its approach, suited my blow to the bellwethering of its paws. My doubts flowed back. Spindrift. Relief. Deep breath. I felt armed once again. I was going to sic the disaster of a lightning bolt on it. I was there with it. Here I am, there you are. But (... *A-a!* ...) the sound of the paws ceased. Bang *flap!* and period. *The monster had stopped short to stand still.*

The Master had no idea what to do anymore. He heard his dog running in the distance. He knew it was on the right track. By going in that direction, he hoped to find the animal again, or be found by it. So, the Master walked straight ahead. But he was burdened by the gravest of solitudes. It let go of the trees to settle weightily on his shoulders. His steps were heavy. His steps were slow. His steps were guilty. He did not know whether it was fatigue or truly the mystery of those trees that was torturing him so. Nothing evil there. The Master perceived instead a virginity outside of morality, something primordial that had been offended, and that had been lost to people from that time on.

That was it. That was surely it. *These places had known damnation.* It was there. Prowling around him. He imagined that it was emanating from him. And plaguing him. He did not understand. He had fought so hard to clear this land, beat back the savages, attend to those *nègres*, present to barbarities the beauty of plantations and the sugar sciences. His life had been nothing but courage and suffering, work and exhaustion, fevered thoughts and heartfelt anxieties. And yet, in spite of these fatigues, the Master slept quite badly. He detected in himself tumultuous shames foreign to the courages he deployed or his heroics as a mighty builder. He had ascribed that to the original sin revealed by his Book, but the Masses had brought no peace. Nor had the confessions. The feeling of shame remained coiled on the inexpressible, the unpronounceable, on the invisible and the unavowable – of which he knew nothing. He was proud of himself but that pride, in certain hours, came apart like the finery of a mountebank. He was there, alone among those trees, and those places, and the heroism of the personal chronicle he kept no longer carried much weight. He had handled – it was written down – the conquering tall-sailed ships. He had popped off bombards against Carib* rages. He had buried, beneath conch shells, friends and brothers. He had blasted parrots, smoked the fat of manatees, gulped down the raw eggs of thrushes that ran along the sands. He had wept under exile and fever, worn-out memories and lost letters. He had planted *pétun,** indigo, and then *cannamelle.** He had modified ships to carry *nègres*. He had sold them. He had bought them. He had given them the best of his race. He had raised the highest walls of stone, dispensaries of marble and gothic vaults where grandeurs slumber. And founded the white cities in the mirror of harbors. And planned ports on the tresses of mulatto women. He had cleared the smoking lands, tamed the rivers vomited by the volcano,* pushed back the snakes that interfered with the dreams of the little angels on fountains. He had made Great Houses of shadowy light and clay, raised mills, set up sugar works. Mapped out the useful routes and the signs at crossroads. He had explored the secrets of alcohols and the sweetness of life (with a very pale woman, with a very white arm, beneath a wide-brimmed hat with bobbing lace). He had won, over mangroves and steep slopes, the blest offering of the most fertile fields. He had never wept, or doubted the divine right that sanctified his actions. ... *And yet ooo solitude!* ... This silence grew as he grew older. This lonely poison in the shadow of his victories. This fate that undid his steps. What he had said of the Great Woods in order to kill off marooning possessed him as well. These Great Woods that knew the Before, that harbored the communion host of an innocence gone by, and which still trembled with primal forces – these woods moved him now. They had fascinated the runaway *nègres*. Those had taken refuge there as in a *ventre-manman*, a mother's womb. They wanted to die there rather than fall in a field furrow. Those escapees looked upon the trees as if contemplating a cathedral. They showed them ceremonial respect. And the trees talked to them. He, the Master, had festooned the trees with wickednesses: *Nests of zombies, nests of devils, nests of fevers, nests of vanishments!* Those *baboules*, those lies were churning themselves up unexpectedly in him. The Master felt it now. The Great Woods were powerful. They stripped you bare, through force or misfortune, *à nu rêche*: harsh-naked. Within their shadows, the Master saw himself sunk in shame. He was afraid. His pioneering impulse stalled. His conqueror's stride faltered. He ought not to turn around. Or look around. Or stare at the stakes of light descending from the sky. He ought to cling to his dog. Follow it until death. This dog alone would allow him to survive. So the Master walked all along a penitence.

He was thinking of the old slave. That most faithful among the faithful, who had devoted the best part of his life to him. Betrayal. He did not understand this flight. The old slave had seen him born, had even shown him signs of affection. Had taught him the training of horses, initiated him into the secrets of yellow fruits and fighting cocks. The *vieux-nègre* had never spoken to him, perhaps smiled sometimes, settled for being there, like a solid grounding from pioneering days. The Master no longer knew whether his father had bought him from the clutches of a slaver, or if he'd come up on this Plantation. He had none of the strangeness of *nègres-bossales* born in Africa, or the ordinariness of native *nègres-créoles*. He had always been there. He was called Fafa, or Old-Syrup, no one really knew why. He'd neither had a wife nor given a child. Had never followed the priest's sermons, or sought baptism or the Host, or worn dilapidated boots or shabby hats. At Father's death – the Master suddenly remembered – the old slave had not attended the singing at the wake. He had dug the grave without the sorrow-spectacle of the house slaves. When the Madame was in her death throes (*la Madame-Maîtresse*, a very charitable old Norman lady, who used to take good care of her *nègres*), the old-fellow had not slumbered out below the Great House, or wailed the lamentations that saddened the cabins when she gave up the ghost. Evidence: the Master saw nothing of him, in intimate memories, but a face of *papaya and boredom,** a large *mute* shadow half out of this world, a big silent beast. Yet, no hatred in him. Or menace. Or danger. But no acceptance. That was it. The *vieux-nègre* had not accepted what was done with him. Ever. And yet one had given him everything, graces and favors. He had not been a slave, no, but an old companion. Yes, even that, a very old companion. One had loved him. Betrayal! It was a betrayal.

The Master did not understand above all this energy that seemed to bear him up. Such an old fellow. The mastiff usually caught up with runaways much quicker than this. But the *vieux-nègre* seemed to run faster than the mastiff. Hard to believe. Such an old fellow. Faster than the mastiff. The Master believed himself faced with a miracle and this increased the mystery of these woods that, gently, more and more, were revealing the silences of his soul. The Master, surprised, discovered water flooding his eyes. An age-old water. Salt water. A slightly bitter water.

The monster had stopped. In some place behind the trees. It knew I was there. It knew I was waiting for it. Its killer's instinct detected my presence. I did not move. Time went by some more. I heard nothing. My arms tried to tremble: my imagination was beginning to head out to sea. I was seeing the monster slip behind the tree where I was posted. Yes, it's there on the other side of the trunk. Slinking slowly around it to break my *l'en-bas*-butt. Despite myself, I turned my head, changed position. Again I imagined it on the other side. And even coming from high up. I did not know what to do or which way to turn. My eyes on alert watched in every direction. I ran to shelter beneath a different *pied-bois* to better cover the surrounding area. Peace. Shade, sunniness, leafiness. Nothing else. So then I listened. Ears pricked up. Nose-holes open. Trying to distinguish the rustle of the wild-beast body against raspy lower branches.

Listening hard. Crossing the silence. Hearing. There was as if a pounding of water. A floundering. I understood on the spot: *the wellspring!* ... The mastiff was at the *fondoc* of the marshy eye and it was floundering! It was well and truly drowning! Clawing to death the crumbling banks! Bogging itself down! Coming back up to get bogged down again! ... My arms to the sky: *Hosanna ... O Gloria!* ...

I rushed toward the spring. I reached it swiftly. I saw the dog. It was frightful. Covered with mud gobs. Covered with leaves. Covered with debris. Barely growling, it was struggling in the moving trap. An evil boiling. Its *bidime*-big paws were collapsing the edges, flinging up vines: a mushy soup of muzzle, mired-up eyes, suffocations, *tohubohu*-churning the most ancient of muds. This would disappear for seven–nine seconds to resurface with *cas-et-fracas*, disturbance-and-turbulence. What I saw was dreadful. It looked like a zombie trying to escape a prison of exorcisms. I did not know how to get closer, or dare get close enough to strike its spine. Get its drowning going. Yet I approached, without really thinking about it. The ground gave way, spongy, soft, sucking, famished. In up to my kneecaps, I was still far from the hellish bouillon. So I retreated. I followed the rim of the hole, hoping for a small tongue of solid ground. But my prey was foaming in the *mitan*-middle of the spring. Inaccessible. *Oala*, immediately the monster *s'envoya-monter*, shot-itself-up. A big-mother fish-leap. I saw it whole, arced in the air in the wink of an eye before falling back heavy into the bouillon hole. This dive splattered me with miraculous mud. The enemy was at my mercy. I was crazy-circling around.

I approached on my belly so as not to sink in. But in that position, impossible to strike. So I returned to the edge. I found a low branch to cling to. That way, I got out over the bouillon. And I struck. *Biwoua*. One-handed. *Biwoua*. With my fears, my hatreds, my rage and my longing to live. The mastiff howled like a Seven-headed Beast. Never heard a catastrophe like that. A calamity of tonsillar sounds and muddy smotherings. It bounded again. Its eyes snapped up mine while it was in the air. It discovered me with curiosity. Twisting even beyond belief, it shot its *manman*-muzzle out at me. I saw its fangs gleam amid the formidable foaming. I struck it again. *Biwoua*. Right on a rib, but this was tickling the trunk of a silk-cotton tree. My position allowed no room for a back-swing. I returned instanter to the rim of the hole, resigned to keeping watch on this agony from a distance. And striking the monster should it happen to emerge. My blows had increased its furies tenfold. Its leaps and tortions were more fearsome. A mite despairing. My eyes bulged: I had never seen such an infernal debacle.

Suddenly, in a sulfurous *sault*, the mastiff landed outside the hole. Full on some soft soil swaddled in roots. I saw it laid out long on the uncertain turf. Its paws were whipping up a blackish scum. Its jaws snapped at the void. Suddenly, it grew calm, exhausted. Its body now expressed nothing but breathlessness. Gradually, its respiration slowed while yet remaining deep-drawn. It looked at me. I went round the hole to be across from the animal. Its eyes followed me. We were soon face-to-face, separated by ten yards of turbid matter. The fantastic spring loosed bubbles of sulfur to burst at the surface. The clear water welled up beneath the cracked crusts to spread wide like magical oil. Luminous patches celebrated its sheen. The monster sprawled out, eyes firmly affixed on mine. I was horrified. I knew it was enmired in the muck. I saw its body gently sinking. Even though it was caught there, I was horrified. Probably because of that gaze free from all fear. It stared at me: blood-curdling curiosity. Its problem was not the marshy trap, it was me. And that scared me. Despite its sudden calm and breathlessness, its energy came through intact.

I knelt down to see it better. I set my eyes to stare and bared my teeth. Had to impress it. Suggest to it (myself as well) that I did not fear it, that I could take or spare its life. We stayed like that in a time without length. Eyes in eyes. It, ever calmer; me, petrified by my show of valiance, plus a *cacarelle*. The Great Woods were moving around me. Became a great blur. I was floating in a dizzy whirl of aggravations. The spring (with its muds, its virgin waters, its hundred-thousand-years-old sulfur) was joining forces with that vision, increasing its giddiness. I found myself laid out in the leaf litter, my gaze level with my enemy's eyes. Eyes in eyes. No blinking. Hold on. Hold *raide*. I appointed myself a hunter, transformed the other into prey. It (I felt this) kept itself opaque; me, my awareness became clouded. The miasmas of the spring must have been poisoning me. So were the monster's eyes, open onto holes-without-end. The animal was stronger than I was. I heard knocking in my chest. My heart wanted to crack open my ribs. I shivered. I moaned. The monster howled. I jumped up *flap*, and fled at top speed. I had lost my bet.

The monster leaped toward terra firma. It knew instinctively where that was. It landed heavily on the edge of the bank. Crawled along a deep furrow. It was managing to get out. I returned frantic to where it was heading. There, I saw it one more time before me. Frothing muzzle. Gaze *sans-maman*. I felt myself weaken. It was creeping toward me as if not fearing me. The muck and dead leaves transformed its skull. It seemed a subterranean crab churning the earth. I struck with every strength. *Biwoua. Biwoua.* My legs, plunged in the sludge, were tipping me off-balance. My wobbly blows were not slowing the terrible advance. I thought the Unnameable was back, so closely did that reptile ramping blend with the viscous soil. A cold resolve was expelling it from the spring. Gazing straight at me, its eyes soon overwhelmed my mind. I lost the courage to strike. Feeble, I aimed blows it deflected with its muzzle. The vise of its jaws gripped my club. I fell to my knees in the slime. I could do nothing. My resistance was giving it leverage to advance more quickly. Pulling on my club was hauling it toward the shore. I gave up. Rolling over, I ran away. Fear severed the suction around my ankles.

Running. I shot my body through the undergrowth, battered myself against tree trunks, got twisted by branches. I was truly throwing myself. It was all leaps, jumps, rolling downhill, sudden somersaults. I was a *tête-folle nègre*, crazy-head beyond control. My legs shot off like wild arrows. My arms flailed the air in impossible flight. I went zigzagging, *zinzolant*. I even thought I went *tourner-virer*, whirly-turning, which worsened my shit-fit. This panic ceased at the sudden snap. *Crac*. A stump. My ankle. The tip-over. I wound up demolished on the ground. Numbness, then *raide* throbbing. A sunburst of pain. I tried to get up. I fell back again. An *andièt-sa* – hateful-clit-hole – swallowed me into its darkness.

The mastiff had not understood what had happened. It had been right on track. The trail had become unbelievable. The scents were thinning out beneath the array of forces in motion. Waves that scintillated, invisible. Shrill sounds, chopped into a complex rhythm and then flowing in discordant sonorous sheets. The mastiff was receiving a real rush of mantras face-on. Its lolling tongue was capturing tastes impossible to know. They awakened chessboards of reveries. The animal took the taste of salt copper then bayberry salve then a rock crystal dissolved in hydromel.* It took a country savanna-liking for guavas then fern seed. It believed it was following a crowd bathed in pollens of exodus, beings of all natures, all odors, all fears, all wills and wants. It sped up: the prey was getting closer. It was there, moving like a *pluie-fifine*-drizzle. The mastiff snarled in surprise. The trail opened immense as a cyclone wind. Whirling in gold and fire. The mastiff thought it had caught up with a giant. The creature pursued was a ball-of-powers. This perplexed the animal: the trail became a maze of mirrors and brutal reversals full of smells in disorderly flight. *As if the being – or beings – pursued were heading back toward it*. At a fine clip. A light authority, sure of itself. The mastiff suddenly felt hunted. Its course became that of an anxious animal. A quiver ran through it. Unpleasant. It tried to move away from the magnificent wake, curve around to better pounce from behind on what was bearing down on it, but the ground vanished. Water. A hole of water pulled the dog down.

It went down deep. The animal, which had crossed rivers and floods, tackled inlets of demented seas, able to cleave difficult currents and explore underwater ravines, knowing water without fearing it, did not understand into what phenomenon it had fallen.

It was a sinkhole.

It was made of water rock fire earth wind and roots. A lively bowel primed for digestion. A dangerous door: *la-porte*. The mastiff felt threatened. It let loose. Battles. Jumps. Sucking-snappings. It needed to bound toward the odors of good earth floating all around. It was leaping with a hint of despair. In the air was when it saw or, rather, sensed, smelled its prey. Its eyes were clogged with vegetal matter. It glimpsed a shape. Radiating an incredible force. *A crystal of light*. This being landed a blow. Weak. Then another. Without using the intensity shining within. If that potential were to mobilize, the mastiff knew it was lost. So it shot its muzzle out at the being. In vain. The shape became a vivid reddish glare. Then a dark pulsation. Fearing a counter-attack, the mastiff leaped up several times until it fell upon a sliver of stable mud bank. The animal began to crawl. And there again, it saw, in its murky vision, the formidable being loom ahead. A prism of lunar clarities and with darkness replete. The being had changed into pure energy. The mas-tiff crept toward this splendor. Attracted by it. Blows landed on the dog but so feebly that they must not have come from the marvel to which it was crawling. Yet the marvel was striking the blows. Probably in ritual defiance. The animal was discovering a worthy adversary. This reawakened the flesh-eating ferocity that exploded inside it in moments of peril. It clamped its jaws on what was hitting it. The thing resisted, then fell apart in its fangs. The mastiff hauled itself over to solid ground where it could stand up. Ready to go wild. But the splendid being was gone. The mastiff thought it had been a hallucination. Yet the trail was there. Quickly recovered. Flamboyant. Quite close. The mastiff shook itself; then, with most prudent paws, padded along it.

*

I woke up *flap*. Pain. It was flaring out from my ankle. I sat up over my leg and thought myself dying. It was broken. A horrible angle. A point of magic whiteness stuck out of a wound. My bone. Blood was frothing fleecily to the top of my thigh. This sight fed my suffering. With scraps of shirt, I tied myself a tourniquet at my knee. I had to pop my leg back into position. I did so shrieking. Quickly. Agony. Deadly dizziness. With two dry sticks I made myself splints. Immobilizing the break in a wrap-tight of little vines. Then I crawled away fast as I could. Twisted earthworm, all tangled up, pitiful. Foundering in a feeling of danger. The monster was coming toward me. It had escaped the trap of the spring and was heading for me. Without running. It approached slowly. With caution or certainty. It knew I was at its mercy.

6. THE STONE

Cette pierre est une roche: this stone is a rock. It grew big in the sea depths, like a greened cannonball.

It rolled into the Atlantic fault where the unknown thing pulsates, it shifted the continental plates, it made us quake from the quaking of our red lands, and it's true, it gave birth to the dog.

This *béké* would be named La Roche, or Laroche, depending on the fickle mood of the ferns of Balata. Is he the same one who made talk with Longoué? Be that as it may, I predict that he knew Oriamé l'Africaine,* and Marie Celat who tells stories. And now they enter this story here to raise the great wind* of the crests.

They stalk *la trace*, to give voice in this night.

Memory of the bones,
sole trace signaling
lives and deeds long gone.

Touch,
folio VI

My leg was heavy. Sometimes, it became light. Numb. Then fires would stir it up. I had to stop slithering to writhe in pain. I was making progress rather quickly in spite of everything. I would slide under the arms of the roots, through the hollows in the fern banks, in the fabulous humus that almost covered me over. I longed to disappear into it. To bury myself as well. I envied these roots penetrating, far, into the soil. They plunged underground the better to reach the sky. I strove to empty my mind the better to resemble them. Forward. Forward.

My hands clutched everything, scooping out earth, tearing leaves from low branches. With the strength of my wrists, *je m'envoyais-aller*, I got myself going. My shoulders and arms were working; the rest was simply surrendered to exhausted sufferings. I possessed, on the other hand, an extreme lucidity. My mind had deployed like a mango tree in bloom. It inhaled the storm of a sky laden like black earth. I was separated from my body; from time to time, whipping pains reminded me of its – distant – presence. The collapse opened within me by the wound had gone away; it no longer frightened me. I tended to it as to a familiar yaws sore. My crawling continued to distance me from my body. I was dragging it as an undone chrysalis. I was going toward another world.

The air had turned heavy, more humid, hot as hell's armpits. The shade rose from the roots and stagnated halfway up the trunks. Solar brilliance blazed in the forest canopy, then sifted luminescence down on the curves of shadows. I was haloed by sky-blue mists. I was cold. I discovered orchids and a fern flower. The fern flower. I had never seen one. It only appears, Word has it, at midnight on Fridays, for thirty-three seconds, and is of a *clair-de-rouge* redshine that can illuminate its surroundings. There, I found it to be of a yellowish blue threaded with steel green. A sumptuous creature. A prodigy of minute equilibria and poise. The fern flower. There it was. Able to grant invisibility, to defuse any *quimbois*-spells. It could in falling reveal the sanctuary of a *béké*'s treasure, or enrich those who carry it for seven days seven times in a row in the heaviness of their hearts. It could baffle for life anyone who trod on it. What sign was this? Another extraordinary circus from my crazy-head? I tried to pick it. My hand hovered forever at the edge of its sepals. My fingers shook. I had always disdained flowers, neither picked nor offered nor sniffed them. My glances had ignored them, but there, I was moved less by pretty words than by the flower itself. A sunny *embellie*. I withdrew my hand, moved off with regret, catching myself staring at it as I hauled my body through the fog without finish and the glacial shade. I was happy to have seen it. Or to have believed that I had.

I did not see the Stone right away. I had advanced as quickly as possible. The feeling of danger prodded me on. I had slipped into whatever was darkest, narrowest, the most tortuous; I had wallowed in decomposition to derail the tracking of my executioner. I had tackled the immense roots of an unknown tree, its ebony foliage leaving not-a-chance to the powdery lights, which fell there as into an abyss, while the surrounding duskiness was foundering against it. I'd had to hoist myself up, and-then let glide, and hoist myself again over a root, and fall again in a forever way. The ground went sloping. I was able to speed up without taking a *solibo*-tumble.* I clung to the riots of lianas and *vermicelles-diable*.* I went down down down. I even feared (so steep was the slant) slipping again toward the maw of a spring. But the bottom of a ravine welcomed me.

A ravine of wonderment.

Regent of eternity.

Center of luminous shades.

Foliage was its sky, journeys of stars pierced by shimmering brilliancies. Everything seemed alive and dead to the hilt. I had entered the most intense stillness of these Great Woods. My mind grew calm, or rather, loosed itself a little more from my body. The fear of death invaded me. I called upon my now familiar pains, unbearable but as human as the fatigue of a lifetime. My sufferings, ooo my flesh!

My eyes still looked up. As if in imploration. As if in adoration. The leaves of the tall trees, liquefied by the mists and the pinpoints of radiance, stretched over the ravine in an opaque and entrancing halo thronging with stunned-looking insects. *Bêtes-à-diable.** Butterflies. Spiders. Yellow-tailed dragonflies. *Touffaille*-swarms of flies and *Yen-yen* midges. Clusters of bats distorted the wild potato vines. At times, gray trembler songbirds, down from the heights, would suddenly appear in a tizzy, then rush back up to melt away in the light. I thought I recognized the water-loving *Cra-cra*, the ringed kingfisher; *Carouges*, shiny cowbirds, nestled under maternal leaves; *Siffleurs de montagne*, rufous-throated solitaires; *Colibris-madère*, purple-throated caribs, a hummingbird whose plumage, at certain angles, flashed lightning. I was covered by a cloth of silence, comforted by languid ferns. I crawled along the ravine. It grew narrower. Abruptly I could go no farther.

A mass was blocking my way.

*

It could have been a tree but it climbs toward no brightness. No foliage augments it. The thing is compressed, compact, dense with itself, related more to the earth. I think I am standing before a root, but the mass is uniform, mossy, without the ruggedness of centuries-old bark. I don't feel that it's lifeless. I'm scared. Believing myself before a legendary monster, a Seven-headed Beast or Dragon of initiatory fears. My uneasy mind loads this mass with all kinds of emanations and interprets them in a way not good. I dread the return of the agonizing visions of my initial escape. Nothing suddenly appears. I lean back against the thing, breathless, wondering how to get around it.

Immense, it disappears into the undergrowth. I clear brush along the side to make my way. Its flanks are embedded in the walls of the ravine. I am caught-there. Impossible to climb over: my leg, my so-heavy body, the worn-out of my arms. I collapse against it like an empty guano sack. Neither sadness, nor discourage, nor despair. I am empty, run ragged, used up. My skin smooths against the ancient moss and feels life in the venerable block. Its density. Unfathomable thicknesses. It is – I understand this now – a *bombe-volcan* sent soaring in very ancient times. A stone. I touch it. Cold. Warm. Vibrant in the faraway of its heart. The ages have covered it with a true shivery skin beneath my feverish fingers. No doubt I have fallen mad: I believe myself slumped against a living stone. I feel it; my palm crumbles the substances; the stone warms up, fissuring the shell of a cemeterial solitude. The stone is friendly. I open my arms to hug it, or to cling to it like a laminated lamina, and I close my eyes.

Borne by a mellow languor. *Marigot*-marsh of fatigues. A kind of drowsiness. I dreamed. Without really knowing of what. Images. Sounds. Gestures. *Siwawa*-abundance of bats with folded wings. Solar frogs at the dawn of time. I have open eyes, but the dream goes on. It's the Stone. *La Pierre qui rêve*: the Stone that dreams. Whackings. Gougings. Ritual breaths. Sacrifice-agonies. Hammered-gold platelets deifying nostrils. Grottoes peopled with cotton forms of humans with eyes of Job's tears.* White vases harassed by an intimate rust. Three-pointed stones instructed in the three last mysteries. Sculpted conch shells set out as guardians. Jars sealed on pensive skeletons. . . . These volutes scroll in my mind. They superimpose themselves on other undulations. I think I see groups of men in anxious migrations, crossing deltas, braving high seas in hollowed-out trees, rebounding on chaplets of islands. They swallow live shellfish and treat the shells as jewelry, they arrow-spear *waliwa*, rock grouper, or trap *chatrou*-octopus in woven-willow jaws. When the welcoming shores rise above underwater drop-offs, they plant *manioc-bois*, dig up roots, and smoke-dry agoutis, iguanas, and beautiful birds. They are from the *Grandes-terres* and the islands. They have seen the world with smaller seas, and their footsteps have trod the stone of the abysses of these times. They leave the way one shatters a destiny, travel along the trail of the straying gods and the paradises their legends keep alive. But they encounter only wars and hatreds, the furious waves of their own madness washing over the follies gone before.

The Stone dreams. It beguiles me with its dreams. I press myself against it, with greedy hands. My mind abandons its marks. It is possible that I speak to it, that I myself am talking to a stone. Or dreaming with it. Yes, our dreams intermingle, a tie-up of seas, savannas, *Grandes-terres* and isles, attacks and wars, dark ship's holds and migrant wanderings over a hundred thousand times a thousand years. A coming together of exiles and gods, failures and conquests, bondage and death. All that – a grandiose *hail!* – whirls in a movement of life: life alive on this earth. The Earth. We are all the Earth.

My convulsive palm wears away the moss. I feel forms beneath my fingers. Incised shapes. Circles. Lines. Patterns of squares. Meanderings spelling something. I scrape what surface I can reach. The Stone is engraved all over. Vulture heads. Broad-cast sowings of dots and interlaced lines. Frog's-feet and labyrinths. Human and animal forms subjected to invisible forces. Tortoise-necks and frigate-bird-heads. Lines and spirals, double crosses, triangles and crosshatchings. My eyes halt at these forms but there I divine fundamental words, sacred gestures and conjurations. Not one crumb of the Stone has remained virgin. The whole hums in all directions like a tattoo on living scales. The engravers succeeded one another for times-without-times. Neither the same peoples, nor the same tools, nor the same intentions. A *ouélélé*-tumult of myths and Geneses. I plumb them with a finger sensitive as a blind man's.

The Stone is Amerindian. These people had inhabited this country for an et-cetera of time, and carved stones this way in the Great Woods. I had learned of their extermination. Old Caribs had taught me about plants, fish without venom, and companion roots. They had unfolded (for me, who cared so little) the narratives of their people: the times before-time, the first times, the lost times – a long thread of words that attempted to fulfill the universe. They had clung to floating gestures and fallen words. They had evoked for me the lands that surrounded this one, and so many other auspicious peoples in homelands more vast. They had murmured to me hopes and despairs, unreal laments, mummified liturgies, useless memories, knowledges undone. I had wanted them to teach me how to survive right where I was, but they discoursed on their past being, at the center of all things. I had not listened. Youth. Here, now, I hear all that again. The Stone does not speak to me; its dreams materialize in my mind the speech of those dying ones I had forsaken. The Stone is many peoples. Peoples of whom only it remains. Their only memory, repository of a thousand memories. Their only word, great with all words. Cry of their cries. The ultimate matter of these existences.

Boulder of heady intoxication. These vanished ones live in me by means of the Stone. A chaos of millions of souls. They tell stories, sing, laugh. Some want to support me, others to question me. Festive presences, emotional, fragile, quick; others, behind the pride of something sacred, more menacing. I perceive feminine graces, artful in drawing near me. I wander in the tumult of a cartload of impossibles. Dumbfounded. I no longer feel the wounds hacking up my body. I have reached a rib of alliance between life and death, victory and defeat, time and immobility, space and nothingness. I embrace the Stone as a refuge-being. I press it against me. I want to dissolve myself there and let nothing of my flesh survive. That is when I see the monster again.

It had come up the ravine. Had stopped. A few yards from me. Looking at me. I lean back on the Stone, rejoining the torment of my leg, the fire of my wounds. But I want to see it. My back against the Stone, I am soothed. *Pièce désespoir*: no despair. No longing for a death in the fangs of my executioner. No, I desire only to see this creature that has tormented me during this run, the meaning of which I do not understand. The animal has gone where I have gone. It is a part of this. The monster observes me as well. Believing strongly in itself. Then, it advances. Gaze on fixed point. It is stained with mud, sweat, and crumpled petals. *Vermicelles-diable* are knotted to its paws. It drags them like medusa hair. Its coat is now too difficult to see. Mosses, orchid pistils, pineapple plant fibers have grafted themselves into its fur. It resembles those idols on which sacrificial materials have transmuted into unspeakable, unnameable things. It approaches me like an inanimate mass, very dense, opaque. I perceive nothing of it, either in waves or sounds. The chantey of the Stone is within me. It fills me with an *évohé** of life.

The being was powerful. Too powerful. The monster had followed the trail cautiously. Its old ferocity, its taste for wars and perils, had reached a virulent pitch. As the trail had changed, this ferocity had crept back to its cradle. Like a brute of the first ages returning to its underground cave. The trail was no longer a field of forces or lights. It had become intoxication. Mixture of ether and horizons. An endless vertigo that annihilated the ground. The monster was following this furrow without really knowing how. Nothing of its ferocity was now in play. It advanced toward this mystery like a shepherd's dog.

It comes within two yards of me. It stares at me in an indescribable way. I have the impression that it's planting itself on the edge of a precipice. It takes another step. Then another that leaves it at a dead set. The monster awaits I don't know what. My tourniquet has come apart. My blood bubbles up around the broken bone. The smell of my wound awakens none of the executioner's zeal. The dog is an indecipherable block. I don't know what to do. No strength left to raise an arm, grasp a branch, try again to split its skull. A faint idea occurs to me. Grab a sharp flint and cut its throat as it leaps. My frozen fingers fumble the dirt. I am not afraid. I do not really want to fight. I am possessed by an indestructible life.

The Master was lost. He no longer heard his dog. He did not know in what quarter to seek it. He was advancing toward something impossible to put right. The old man had perhaps cut the animal's throat. The Master put that quickly out of mind for it was impossible. That dog was a Beast-of-war. And slaughter. It was used to the ways of these *nègres*. Besting it was not of this world. And yet, the Master was afraid. This silence and this quandary worried him. He walked straight ahead praying that his dog had kept going in this direction. But he felt lost past all return. He told himself that these woods would swallow him up, that their murmurings would soon lead to damnations, that gargoyles would be born of the shadows to sing to him of his shame. The Master had not ceased weeping. Without much knowing why or wherefore, he had cried like a little child. No one could see him, so his rank and manners were tumbling from the highest sky, and his tears flowed freely. He attempted to make them mean something. He was crying, he told himself, for those who were not crying, over what had not moved him, over what he had not seen, over caresses impossible to give, over the paltriness of the foundations he had believed imposing. He was crying over the triumphant failure that had been his life. At times, he pulled himself together. Declared himself the victim of moody hallucinations. Certain plants possessed venomous juices. Those resins must be poisoning him. He kept telling himself that, but he knew his distress came from within and knew how forcefully these magnificent trees fostered revelations.

I seek me that weapon. Then admit this is only a reflex of my flesh. Which I can shed. So then, I open my fingers. I return my forearms to the welcome of my knees. I apply myself to breathing as on certain evenings before my cabin – after the rain – when I felt good. Plowing back those times so rare when I felt good. Little moist moments, gentled heart on its own, hush-there mouth, and sweet breeze. But the commotion of the Stone reappeared in me, violent and symphonic. It reawakened the agitations that have possessed me. A dance of inner celebration breaks out. Exploding sheaves of birds. Flights of tattered butterflies in ecstasy. Risings to the rhythm of the drums. Orders to the rain. Loving injunctions to fertile females. Submissions to the sun. Miseries of possessions in the circle of flames. Effronteries in the offering of silks on a belly. Numbers chatting where the water rejoins its bed. Destructions of limits. . . . *Celebrations! Celebrations!* I am pleased, lord of dances, by this ebullient disharmony. By this modest immoderation. Yet all this takes place within an infinitely tiny part of me. What I call 'me' can also dwell in an infinitesimal part of what I perceive. Or receive. I am neither active nor passive. Neither in volition nor in coma. A non-ordinary state, at the other end of this world but with which I can live this world, this broken leg, this poor wrinkled body, this pitiless monster tensed in front of me. Without knowing why, I want to offer myself a name. Assign myself a name as at the hour of the baptisms ordered by the Master. I find nothing. *There are so many names in me.* So many possible names. My name, my Great-name, ought to be able to cry them all. Sound them all. Count them all. Burn them all. Render them all justice. But that is not possible. Nothing is possible for me anymore. Everything is beyond necessary and possible for me. Beyond justifiable. No *Territory** is mine, or language, or History, or Truth is mine, but all that is mine at the same time, to the limit of each pure term, to the far reach of their concerted melodies. I am a man.

I believe I am weeping but weeping makes no sense. I believe I still feel a pang, or even a shiver of fear when the monster comes closer to me. But all that is only a reflex of flesh. Insane muscle memories. Fixed feeling in my bones. My bones. What will they say about me? Like those peoples sheltering in a stone, I will end up as a few lost bones in the depths of these Great Woods. I see them already, those bones, architecture of my mind, substance of my births and deaths. Some will make dust, others rocks. Some will sculpt themselves shapeless, others will dream of crystal and singing flutes. Some will form a shell over the mystery of a pearl, others will go the invariable way of circles unbegun and reluctant to end. But that is not important: my saliva tastes like dawn. The monster, they say, drew nearer. Fetid muzzle. The man was not even surprised when the enormous face reached his own.

The monster did not believe its eyes. Its prey was mingling with a stone teeming with a myriad of peoples, voices, sufferings, outcries. Unknown peoples were celebrating an awakening. The being seemed like lightning shooting through the Stone. An un-shining energy. It did not project itself anywhere. It did not affect the reigning eternity. An incandescence pulled-in to its very core. The monster drew still closer. It perceived things that its mind could not envisage. It soon dismissed its own memories. It put aside the mass of its instincts where its behaviors were dozing. It gave itself over to what it was receiving. It looked on in the way one watches, from the height of a chasm, the dusk of a star, or the great-work of its birth. It was not too sure. The monster went even closer to the being and, without much knowing why, with all the conviction available to it, began to lick it. The monster did not lick blood, or flesh, or the sweat of flesh. It garnered little taste. It was licking. That was the only gesture he was given.

*

The dog reappeared. The Master did not even start with pleasure. The animal came toward him and the Master did not know him. He had loosed a killer; returning to him was an enormous animal, too serene and too quiet. The Master knelt down and hugged him. He held him tight the way one clasps a corpse to bring it back to life. But the mastiff had changed. His eyes were lively. His eyes were shining. His musculature was still, almost soft. Then, the Master wept for the monster he had lost.

He followed the animal heading back down to the Plantation. A melancholy fell upon the Master. It made pleasant those woods abandoned with an irremediable step. He did not feel he was returning empty-handed, having lost a *nègre* or been made mock of by an ingrate of a Maroon. He was returning bearing something he could not name. His fatigue had disappeared; the shame and fear had melted away. The tears had dried on his face but above all, within him. In him, now, other spaces were bestirring themselves, spaces where he would never go, perhaps, but where one day no doubt, in a future generation, hopefully in the full radiance of their purity and legitimate strength, his children would venture, as one confronts a first misgiving.

7. THE BONES

Today the laboring in the cane fields pushes their rusted nudity all the way to the dark green of the heights. What was retreat, trembling, furor of being and smoke of charcoaled wood gives way little by little to fertilizer. The histories, the stories, the doubles, become fewer, come together. The times are given one to the other. Yet who returns to the slope of the morne and digs in the earth?

Shapeless shape of the bones,
invincible intention of the creative will.

Touch,
folio VII

The bones were found in the backwoods. *Vieux-nègres* very
often come to show me *l'antan*, time-gone-by. The *Marqueur
de Paroles** – Word Scratcher – is for them a guardian of the
past. Governor of memories. Giver of nostalgias for times
and epochs, certainties and identities. They've offered me
antique objects; showed me things of some age; proposed
their lives to me for writing down and their exploits for the
telling. The one who spoke to me of the Stone was a *vieux-
nègre-bois*, an old man of the forest. He secretly rummaged
up the refuse all-around in the *béké* woods. I'd met him in
the town of Morne-Rouge,* during a pilgrimage I never miss.
I love that *bombe populaire* – a throng of festive (and fervent)
humanity – around the church and the steps of the calvary.
I love those folks in their Sunday best who let their chains

drift with the street* and sell any-and-everything. I had never paid attention to the religious aspect of this holiday. I am not fond of crowds, yet this encounter respected and nourished my solitudes. I had drunk three-caterpillar absinthe* with the *vieux-nègre-bois*. He had talked about my books – which he had never read and never would. Had congratulated me for that *antan* restored to the country. I was at the time finishing a work* about a neighborhood in Fort-de-France, a poor epic that was taking me forever-and-ever and leaving me all at sea. I was explaining this to him (probably to alleviate boredom) when he spoke to me about a stone.

A Caribbean stone.

He had found it and no one else but he would be able to find it. It was *ancienne au dépassé*, he said: older than timeless. It was too *magique* to *critique*, he said. *Magnifique sympathique*. He proposed that I should see it. I was a bit interested in the Caribs. Some knowledgeable friends used to offer me information useful to my little projects. I was set on finding out how a vanished people could inhabit us, in what way and what mystery. But all of them – really serious anthropologists, devotees of science – turned down the adventure into this poetic muck. They willingly left it to me. I did not agree to go see the Stone. Or else, I went there with him but he did not find it anywhere. Or else, one of my brothers went there and saw it in my place. Or else no one saw it, except that *vieux-nègre-bois* who probably talked too long to me about it. Unless it was my brother.

A volcanic rock. Imagining it astonishing. Covered with Amerindian signs. Guapoïdes. Saladoïdes. Calviny. Cayo. Suazey. Galibis. Every epoch jostling there together. I would have come upon it in some surprise. I had seen one in the forest of Montravail, in the commune of Sainte-Luce, but this one was doubtless in no way comparable. The Stone was supposedly in a deep ravine, way off on its own. Doubtless a ceremonial site. The *vieux-nègre-bois* spoke (to me or I don't know whom) of another discovery. He had looked carefully around the Stone, doubtless seeking some of those treasures that harass our dreams. And he had found bones. Human bones. He showed me a sliver wrapped in oiled paper along with an old rosary. I saw it. I looked at it. I touched it in spite of his warnings about evil spells. He himself said he didn't know why he was keeping that bone splinter. He had promoted it to a *garde-corps de chance*, a good-luck bodyguard. A relic to ward off misfortune.

I often went back to be near that stone. In dreams. Above those bones. In dreams. After distressing days my dreams go marooning. In these dreams, I lean back against the Stone. I contemplate the jumbled heap of bones. Who could that have been? A Carib. Doubtless. A Carib shaman who would have lived there, who would have engraved his memorial accounts and sunk himself into old age. Or the bones of a man wounded in initiatory fervor come to die in the sanctuary. My mind drifted like that around the Caribs.

I imagined the bones. I saw them as eerie. Fossilized. No skull. A femur.

The clavicles. Some vertebrae. A few small formless bits. Porous things. And a broken tibia the *vieux-nègre-bois* had mentioned, or maybe it was my brother. Those bones were loaded. A mute cry with no way out. I felt this yet could not express it. What did they have to tell me? And why was I returning to them so often in these dreams? We have so few intact memories. They have worn away, drifting in tangles, and have never been indexed: there was a reason for those bones to trouble me. They could have been from anyone among us. Amerindian. *Nègre. Béké. Kouli.** Chinese. They spoke an entire epoch, but one open in its uncertain totality. *I should not have touched that relic.*

One day, imagining the broken tibia, I thought of the *nègres marrons.* That ravine was a fine refuge for a runaway slave. My *nègre marron* would have gone through the Great Woods, would have been wounded, would have come to die right over that stone. I felt what he would have experienced in that place, so far from everything, by that stone with those carvings that beggared all imagination. *Roye,* alas! *I should not have touched that garde-corps charm.* I was the victim of an obsession, the most distressing, exhausting, and familiar one, the sole escape from which is Writing. To write. I thus realized that one day I would write a story, this story, molded from the great silences of our mingled stories, our intermingled memories. About an old man slave running through the Great Woods, not toward freedom: toward the immense testimony of his bones. The infinite renaissance of his bones in a new genesis. *I should not have touched anything.* I will try to model my *vieux-bougre* through a folktale parlance and a runner's wind. A parlance that would have its say while I show it silent. A parlance that would mix the muteness of his tongue with the dominative blows that crushed his speaking. A language without high or low, absolute in its will, open in its principle. My old-fellow-slave would set out compact and hardened; would open like great wind. *O I shouldn't have.*

I conserve the un-intelligible in the Stone and the bones. Obsession. The *vieux-nègre-bois* is my accomplice, his *gardecorps* envelops me. As for my brother, he is waiting for me to write a Caribbean tale. He has some word-bits he slips me sometimes. I urge him to write them up himself. He doesn't dare. Writing is *raide*, he says. I grant him that too quickly. But I had penetrated to the depths of the land. Counted. Indexed. Touched on healthy admirations. Hauled out lost imaginations, the yet-to-comes and the at-present of forgotten times. I now knew we were hurtling toward life, full in the heart of our bones, facing the Great Woods of the world busy binding itself together. Great Woods of the peoples who bond as brothers, *Territoires qui font Terre*: Territories that make Terra, tongues that hail harmonies. We are all, like my runaway old-fellow, pursued by a monster. To escape our old certainties. Our so-careful moorings. Our cherished reflexes clock-timed into systems. Our sumptuous Truths. In a heady rush toward the unforeseeable to-be-constructed that opens its dangers to us. Confronting this chaos, tackling this task, understanding this intention and following it through. Such Writing is *raide*. The old slave had left me his bones, meaning: cartload of memories-histories-stories and eras gathered together. I imagined his last struggle, his ultimate *huh* of effort. That broken leg had dispelled his illusion about his run, pointing out (with a fearsome point) the *clearing* of his mind. They were warrior's bones, says my so-genial brother. Of a warrior unconcerned with conquest or domination. Who would have been on the run toward another life. Of sharing and transformative exchanges. Of the world's humanization in its wholeness. Doubtless possible. But my good fellow could also have *quite simply run*. A lovely run, completely meaningful in its very simple beauty, and thus open when touched by infinity. Very often, with the dream of that stone, musing on that tibia, I free myself from my militant concerns. I take the measure of the matter of bones. Neither dream, nor delirium, nor fanciful fiction: a vast detour that goes even to extremes to return to the combats of my age, bearing the unknown tablets of a new poetry. Brother, I shouldn't have, but I touched the bones.

December 1996
Diamant–Morne Rouge–La Favorite

TRANSLATOR'S AFTERWORD: ÉDOUARD GLISSANT AND PATRICK CHAMOISEAU

All quotations are my translations from the French texts in question, for which any available English titles are also given.

In 1635, Pierre Bélain d'Esnambuc arrived in Martinique with about a hundred French settlers, and by 1660, the resident Caribs had essentially been 'disappeared' into history. The growing colony made sugar its main product and trading commodity. In 1685 Louis XIV, the Sun King, promulgated the Code Noir to regulate the transportation of Africans into slavery on sugar plantations in the French colonies. Several hundred years of slavery – and brutal slave rebellions – then carried on through the French Revolution (the French Convention abolished slavery in 1794, at least in theory) and Napoléon (who as consul re-established slavery in 1802), to end at last with the complete abolishment of slavery on French territory in 1848.

Napoléon's about-face on slavery is widely imputed to his wife, Joséphine, a native of Martinique whose plantation family owned hundreds of slaves. In 1859, a statue of Joséphine, cut from marble donated by her grandson Napoléon III, was erected in La Savane, a park in Martinique's capital, Fort-de-France. In 1991 this statue was beheaded, as was Joséphine's first husband in 1794 during the Reign of Terror. Several years later, red paint was splashed on the neck and shoulders of the statue. As of 2017, the paint and beheaded statue are still there.

After abolition in 1848, Martinique remained a French possession until it was made a *département* in 1946, a *région* in 1974, and – in spite of interest in independence and autonomy on both sides – a *collectivité territoriale* in December 2015.

Martinique is not an independent state.

Patrick Chamoiseau was born in Martinique in 1953, and his books reflect both life there and the way he views his evolution as a writer.

The three autobiographical narratives of his early years are ingenious tales that touchingly expose the pernicious effects of the island's colonial past and dependent present.

Antan d'enfance (*Childhood*) introduces the little *négrillon*, who grows up in Fort-de-France in a family apartment ruled by his indomitable mother, Mam Ninotte. Hungry for knowledge, he explores the riches of his Creole world. Pining for school in *Chemin d'école* (*School Days*), he inaugurates 'the age of petroglyphs' with a stick of chalk: doodling on walls like a tiny Cy Twombly, the Scribbler is born.

The *négrillon*'s first teacher wants his charges to survive in their 'French' society, so, meaning well (and lapsing into Creole himself when exasperated), he tries to suppress their Creole natures, even by hitting them with a switch. When a substitute teacher extolls their African roots to foster racial pride, the children cannot make sense of him, either. The *négrillon* hunkers down 'in this sacking of their native world, in this crippling inner ruination,' and 'without fully realizing it,' *ensures his own survival*: entranced by the mysteries of *ABC*, he studies 'for his own pleasure. Bowed over his pages of writing,[. . .] the pen scritching along,' he becomes an apprentice Word Scratcher.

In *À bout d'enfance*, the narrative complexity of reminiscence intensifies: Chamoiseau speaks directly to himself 'at childhood's end': 'My *négrillon*, where have you gone to ground?' The narrator reflects on the nature of memory, solitude, the border between reality and imagination, and the anticipated promise of writing he had sensed so long ago. The *négrillon* turns to books and dreams for guidance in all things, particularly in the *mastery of the imaginary*. For the challenge this book poses is, how to live? Which will soon become: *how to write?* How to find what still speaks in the past despite the treachery of memory? 'O my *négrillon*, I see myself seeing you,' says the narrator; 'I see you preparing me. . . . ' And 'in a lucidity of dreams, of poetry and of novels, at the very heart of the writing, perhaps intact, always attentive, and even at the tag end of childhood, the child is present.'

By the time this last book in the trilogy appeared, Chamoiseau was the author of an already sizable body of work. After studying law and social economy in France, he had become a social worker there and later in Martinique, where his interest in ethnography and the influence of Édouard Glissant inspired him to study increasingly threatened forms of Creole culture. His first novel, *Chronique des sept misères* (*Chronicle of the Seven Sorrows*), follows the hectic misadventures of a market *djobeur*-porter – a vanishing breed – in Fort-de-France, while *Au temps de l'antan* (*Creole Folktales*) is an homage, as is *Solibo magnifique* (*Solibo Magnificent*), to Creole storytellers and their dying art. From the outset Chamoiseau has tried to portray a Martinique true to the fading authentic realities of an island in sociocultural crisis, a threatened heritage that gives the lie to the image of carefree French citizens untouched by social injustice and racism. Paradoxically, these savage truths are told in language of extravagant invention, through often farcical events and even supernatural tomfoolery that can leave the reader caught between laughter and despair.

In everything he writes, Chamoiseau cherishes the figures of the storyteller, the Maroon, the drifter-wanderer, the Word Scratcher, the warrior of the imaginary, all those who fight against their marginalization on an island where their captured ancestors were dumped to literally slave their lives away making money for their torturers, so well might they ask: *Whose country is it, anyway?* In his Goncourt Prize–winning novel *Texaco*, the avatars of resistance swarm in many guises to defend their Creole neighborhood, Texaco, a precarious squatter section of Fort-de-France in a coastal industrial park. Watched over by a *Mentô* sorcerer, the stalwart Marie-Sophie Laborieux, in an epic sweep through time and place, 'pleading our cause,' tells her family history and that of Texaco, highlighting the increasing political awareness by Martinicans of their embattled and sometimes opposing identities as a people. The crazy-quilt polyphony of narrative voices includes the Word Scratcher, Oiseau de Cham,* who will encourage Marie-Sophie by extolling 'the vast weave that is literature, the multiple-and-one clamor gathering together the languages of the world, peoples, lives.' Marie-Louise begins writing in notebooks – and feels a kind of formaldehyde death settle over her careful sentences as she attempts to capture the Creole parlance of her late father. She misses *life* in her words, with their avalanche now cut up by commas, and her dilemma mirrors the author's, for words are air, and how can one trap the wind? As the Word Scratcher noted when this saga began, 'literature in a living place must be taken alive. . . .'

The monumental range and importance of Édouard Glissant's work are beyond summary here, but his major themes are vital to *Slave Old Man*, in which his texts figure so totemically. Arguing for the valorization of black experience everywhere through ancestral ties to Africa, the political and literary movement of Négritude in the 1930s challenged French colonial power in all its forms, and in the Caribbean, condemned acculturation and its acceptance of the 'tourist' myth of the 'happy isles.' In the early 1980s, turning away from this Afrocentric orientation, Glissant formulated the concept of Antillanité, 'Caribbeanness,' which expanded the range of the archipelago to include all peoples historically present in that region, and emphasized the need for those present-day inhabitants alienated by social injustices to reclaim their sense of both *place* and *collective memory*.

Bluntly put, the rigid hierarchies supporting such iniquities as the master/slave, white/black plantation system were denounced by Glissant, who early on endorsed the now-familiar challenge to all such weaponized binary oppositions by attacking their foundation in self-serving Western theories – of knowledge, race, politics, culture, language, history – that can blindly endorse human horrors on the ground. For example, History, the logbook of a dominant culture, often overshadows real human *histories*: in Chamoiseau's *School Days*, a Martinican black child opens a textbook to read: 'Our ancestors, the Gauls. ... ' As Glissant notes in *Le discours antillais* (*Caribbean Discourse*), 'History is not only an absence for us, it is vertigo,' and in his novels history – an occulted history – is the image of black bodies weighted with cannonballs plummeting silently to the ocean floor.

By critiquing those reductive universal truths, Glissant wished to bring thought and imagination more into line with lived reality. Without the colonialist ideals of purity, divine genesis, and other touchstones, 'creolization' ceases to be a dismissive matter of miscegenation, mongrelization, or even simple hybridization and becomes the open recognition *and celebration* of natural variation in all things. Relieved of any concept of identity founded on 'closed' notions of race, territory, or nation, the archipelago in Glissant's thematics now figures as a string of islands in flux, involved in what he saw as the outward influence of the Caribbean Sea toward the Americas and beyond. Glissant was an early advocate of 'Caribbeanness' as a global phenomenon, and his concept of creolization evolved into a continuous process, that of contacts among cultures or elements that produce unpredictable results, new identities. Creolization 'creates in the Americas absolutely unexpected cultural and linguistic microclimates, places where the repercussions among languages or among cultures are abrupt' (*Une pensée archipélique*).

Glissant saw in the malleability of Creole languages a force for diversity, an inherent opposition to any monopolizing, homogenizing sameness. This resistance, protective of difference, he called *opacité*. All languages everywhere are shape-shifters, so to speak, and English is known for its omnivorous appetite for foreign words and homegrown neologisms, but the Creoles of the Caribbean are marked by their violent creation in an unholy crucible. The process of creolization depends on the survival of diversity, of irreducible otherness, of opacity as a mode of pushback against cultural appropriation. Opacity not as obscurity, but as an irreducible particularity, the stubborn otherness of the Other.

The poet, for Glissant, is indeed that *unacknowledged legislator of the world*, capable of transforming history, and although he was never a politician, Glissant's is a political poetics. From *Le discours antillais*: 'The past, our endured past, which is not yet history for us, is yet here tormenting us. The writer's task is to explore this obsessive pain, to "reveal" it constantly in the here and now.[. . .] For my part, for a long time I have been trying to conquer a sweep of time that steals away, to live a landscape that keeps proliferating, to sing a history that is nowhere given. The epic and the tragic have in turn seduced me with their promises of slow disclosure. Constrained poetics. Force-fed language. We all write to lay bare what is at work unnoticed.'

In 1997 Chamoiseau published both *L'esclave vieil homme et le molosse* (*The Old Slave and the Mastiff*) and a book that can be seen as 'theory' to the novel's 'practice': *Écrire en pays dominé* (*Writing in a Dominated Land*), a lively combination of autobiography and theoretical reflection that asks: 'How to write when, morning 'til dreams, your imaginings take nourishment from images, thoughts, values that are not your own? How to write when what you are stagnates outside of the fervors that determine your life? How to write, dominated?'

Suffocating beneath the weight of colonial modernity, a spiritual desert of consumerism, and an avalanche of concrete and cars, the 'poor scribe, Word Scratcher in this broken land,' suspects that 'all domination (the silent kind even more) germinates and develops at the very core of what one is.[. . .] Therefore I had to question my writing, inspect its dynamics, suspect the conditions of its coming-forth, and detect the influences worked upon it by this no-longer-visible domination.'

Reacquainting himself with his birth land after his ten years in France, Chamoiseau embarks in *Écrire en pays dominé* upon an epic review of his life and the history and literature of the West Indies. He tracks his growing awareness of the silent destruction around him, describes his search for information, understanding, and counsel in his reading, which now ranges among the literatures of the world, and reflects on the difficult interface between literature and life. Chamoiseau's text can be as spare as a haiku or as densely tangled as mangrove roots, and includes the Creole call-and-response influence of 'the old warrior,' whose every harangue, warning, taunt, encouragement, nugget of information, and so on is introduced as follows: 'The old warrior gives me to understand: ...'

Glissant's writings, always concerned with the concrete particulars of Caribbean reality, do much to support the theoretical armature of Chamoiseau's review, which is not dryly abstract, but deeply engaged with living. When Chamoiseau reruns those history lessons from his Mam Ninotte childhood, this time he will ditch the Gauls to re-examine the fate of the first inhabitants of the Caribbean archipelago and their almost complete erasure in the onslaught of colonization. He re-catalogues the horrors and complicities of the Triangular Trade, and the post-abolition release of slaves as little more than poverty-stricken refugees on the island where they were born, still bereft of their ancient birthright, stolen centuries before. Even today, although about 90 percent of Martini-cans are of mixed African and European descent, their island's economy remains largely in the hands of people of European ancestry.

All the material benefits Martinique enjoys as part of France cannot mask, for Glissant and his heirs, the spiritual malaise eating away at their island. In a sense, Chamoiseau is conducting a double cultural psychoanalysis, not only addressing the conflicted heart of Caribbean societies but facing his own quandaries as a Martinican writer. Chamoiseau specifically cites Glissant in his discussions of the *originality* of Caribbean 'origins' on islands forcibly or entrepreneurially stocked with peoples from around the world in a virtual laboratory of modern creolization. And by comparing his life to that laboratory, Chamoiseau performs a kind of experiment, testing his mentor's theories in the field, evaluating the purpose of *literature and the writer* in the real world.

While studying and working in France, Chamoiseau had read Glissant's novel *Malemort*, a dense, fragmented Martinican labyrinth of corruption and disillusionment, and been stunned. He understands nothing. When the strangeness of France – the seasons, the snows, the subways 'of ten thousand solitudes' – casts him back almost naked upon himself, memories of his native land overwhelm him; hidden things appear as in 'a fluorescent dream.' The map of his childhood returns to him – and now he rereads *Malemort* with moving clarity as 'the irruption into [French] of another consciousness.' He reads *Dézafi*, a novel in Creole by Frankétienne, 'the father of Haitian letters,' and understands that his Haitian Creole has cracked open its mineral gangue to reveal itself as art. 'I had discovered that intense circulation between the Creole and French languages, and creative freedom in a dominated language.'

When he takes core soundings of the 'anthropological magma,' the layers of Martinican 'selves' (Amerindians, Europeans, Africans, Indians, Asians, Levantines), this time he researches them thoroughly, 'dreaming' himself into their stories, playing their roles, seeing with their eyes. In the end Chamoiseau speaks for a Creole-self. 'I no longer sought for myself any primordial purity but accepted a previously unbearable idea: we were born *in* the colonial coup' that determined our relationship to all that exists, born out of the wombs of slave ships and 'the tremors of islands and continents.'

And of all the figures evoked in this book, the most vital, 'born of that asphyxia, O that strength! – the one who bestowed a Word upon those men of the foundations,' may be the *Conteur Créole*, the storyteller who makes 'lost voices' speak.

Chamoiseau dreams him up:

My body takes on the gestures, songs, dances. I call, speak, and reply to drum, and drum takes flight with my swirls of words.[. . .] I mix men with animals, earth with water, sun and moon, lies with a few varieties of truth, and everything flutters around with everything. I am not alone in speaking, I speak in no one's place, I speak in concert: they get me going, I heckle, they support me, I question, they outrun me, I scoot pass them, they surround me, I get away, they appeal to me, I withdraw, they pull back, I round them up and inquire, they murmur, I improvise.[...] I am in this enlivening dream. And suddenly I understand: the Storyteller makes these bodies, re-energized by movement, *speak-together*, answer-together, stride with the same step, feel the same joys, unanimous fears, all-breaking-away together.

The Storyteller has no Genesis, no History; his parlance comes only from a rebellious cry in that slave-ship hold, which 'endowed that parlance with a hopeless audacity tied to all desires.' Seeking out the old *conteurs'* jousting contests, Chamoiseau admires and records the wordplay, folktales, proverbs, riddles, insults, and especially the 'beautiful jubilation' of their Creole. Yet the *conteurs* are fading away, on an island in thrall to commercial powers and the mother country. 'I had to write with this country, snatched up as a whole, redesigned with my dreams.' But in which language? Chamoiseau now feels he has absorbed the lessons of *Malemort* and *Dézafi*.

'The dominant language, when learned as something outside oneself, keeps its distance: one manipulates it as a petitioner. Wanting to conquer it, one tries to master its orthodox element.' In this way, however, even defiant opposition becomes an observant ritual. 'The colonial Centers had set out their languages like nets.' In trying to write, 'We had found ourselves within them with our motherland languages and our barbarous parlances. Some of us pieced together our native languages to turn them into nets, too. Others tried to launch the triumphant net back at the dominant Center' with more-than-impeccable French.

But 'the languages of the colonial nations have drifted away from their sources and are no longer enough to designate a nationality, an identity, or even to delineate some sort of anthropological correctness.' *The colonial community is now open to all languages, cultures, and peoples.* 'I, an American Creole, found myself closer to any other English- or Spanish-speaking Caribbean than to all other French-speakers like myself, wherever in the world we had landed. Two languages had been given to me, along with the Word of the *Conteur* and his oral literature, and literature with its centuries of writing. I had to call forth in each word, each phrase, that muddled richness, that Diversity within: *what belonged to me.'* Thus used, 'the language in question explodes at the call of individual parlance.'

However, this requires more than creolizing language, playing mix-and-match; it goes beyond 'the solitary Word of the *Conteur*, even the primordial material of his Voice.' Chamoiseau must imagine his own Word, divine his own parlance in the language of choice, and so he appoints himself a Word Scratcher, 'to evoke how much I was setting out across a constant state of fluid change.' Each book he writes becomes an 'unfinished stage of useful explorations,' and his continuing education in world literature leads him to promote himself to Warrior of the Imaginary: 'Hardly more lucid, but lucid regarding the mirage of his lucidity.' ('The old warrior gives me to understand: . . . ooo, you amuse me, you amuse me! You, a Warrior!') Such a Warrior 'brings the ambiguity of the real back into the *opening-up* of the text, the complex of each sentence favoring many an awakening,' so that *all readers will encounter their own individual text*, for 'Writing is not certainty, but discovery.'

The old warrior weighs in at the end: at the heart of life's contrary forces, 'let us be careful to establish our resist-ances, meaning our *equilibria*, to better safeguard the spirit above our Earth, in its superb idea, touched by the distant hum of the Galaxies, and henceforth, for ourselves, in the murmur of a sweet beguine,* let's take our time asking the only worthwhile question: DOES THE WORLD HAVE AN INTENTION?'

– *Linda Coverdale*

NOTES

The terms in question are often given within the entry in their Creole/Kreyol form, to show the difference with French or creolized French. Any translations of quoted French texts are my own.

15 *diablesses* Like most spirits, the she-devil appears at night. She waits in lonely places or goes to dances looking for men to seduce, or sometimes races along a road in a stolen oxcart, shrieking and singing, hunting for souls. Ravishingly beautiful, a *djables* wears long dresses to hide her telltale clattering animal hooves (and is often seen on riverbanks washing huge mounds of white petticoats). When through with a man, she might steal his spirit and break his neck or toss him off a cliff. Survivors of any amorous encounters claim

to have awakened hugging skeletal remains. To ward off a *djables*, smoke a cigarette.

15 **Maître-béké** A *béké* is a white Creole born in the French West Indies, a descendant of the slave-owning colonists from the seventeenth century, and the word is still in use today. A *Met-bétjé* is the master of a plantation. The first permanent colony in Martinique was established by Pierre Bélain, Sieur d'Esnambuc, and the nobiliary particle *de* proclaims him 'Lord of Esnambuc.' In the French text, the author uses the terms *Maître-béké* and *Maître* interchangeably at first, but after the plantation owner's first use of the mastiff, he is referred to only as the *Maître*. To simplify the English text, the *Maître-béké* will be called the Master from now on.

15 **mastiff** The **French** title of this novel is *L'esclave vieil homme et le molosse*: the slave old man and the molosser. Named after Molossus, grandchild of Achilles and ruler of the tribe in Epirus first known for the common ancestor of these animals, the molosser is an ancient type of large, well-built dog with heavy bones, a short, strong neck, and a massive head with a short muzzle and pendant ears. The modern breeds recognized as molossers include many mastiffs, the Great Dane, the Newfoundland, and the Rottweiler.

16 **genocide** Colonial conquest soon wiped out almost all the indigenous Caribbean island populations through

enslavement, European diseases, and active extermination, leaving behind place names like Guadeloupe's
Morne des Sauteurs (Jumpers' Hill), commemorating
legendary mass suicides of Amerindians leaping off
cliffs into the sea.

17   **oil and vinegar** Vinegar was used aboard slave ships
to fumigate the fetid holds and mask the smells of
sickness in the human cargo, who would be rubbed
down with palm oil to make their skin look healthy
before they were sold.

17   *raide* Rèd is a Creole intensifier that can mean:
striking; *pitiless, callous*; *stiff, rigid*; *tense*; *tough*; *hard,
difficult*; etc. It can also be an exhortation to hang on,
not give up, be brave.

18   *veillées* The *vey* is a late-night storytelling gathering
(or, more dramatically, a wake) at which the crowd
sings, dances to drums, bears witness to the life of
the deceased, and participates enthusiastically in the
ritual performances of the skilled Creole storytellers,
whose repertoire ranges from time-honored jokes to
incomprehensible gabble, with sounds that are simply
verbal vibration, brute opacity, or images in which
the *conteur* describes seemingly nonsensical visions
that yet have a method to their madness. When
Chamoiseau's Papa-*conteur* babbles on, for example,
about the mastiff 'at turning points and stream-
boundaries[...] draped in leopard skins,' we would

do well to remember that leopard pelts are the pre-
rogative of African royalty, while folktales around the
world see crossroads as gateways to the supernatural
and waterways as impassable to malevolent spirits.

18 *danse-calenda* The *kalennda* was described by Father
Jean-Baptiste Labat, a Dominican missionary who
at the end of the seventeenth century provided one
of the earliest accounts of slave life in the Antilles.
To the beat of drums, a line of women and a line of
men would repeatedly advance toward one another
and retreat, leaping and pirouetting with 'lascivious'
gestures and improvised songs.

19 *Mentor* A *Mentô* is a senior *quimboiseur*: a magician,
healer, and spiritual guide, and in the hell of slavery,
the plantation *quimboiseurs* offered a vital, if tenuous, connection to all that had been lost during the
Middle Passage. *Quimbois*, like Haitian *vodou*, is an
animist religion, and the *quimboiseur* is a 'master of
knowledge' who deciphers what is occult, not immediately understandable. The superpowerful *Mentô* is
distinguished by his ability to be, in his hidden resistance to enslavement, present yet absent, even within
the plantation.

19 the Before-land A *nègre-guinée* was a slave born in
Africa, and many slaves believed that at death they
would recross the Atlantic to *ginen* (*guinée*, 'Guinea'),
the African homeland they had all lost. Some even

killed themselves to set out sooner. A certain idea of the 'return to Africa' has its own history, notably with Négritude, the movement championed by the celebrated Martinican poet and politician Aimé Césaire, author of the majestic and hugely influential *Notebook of a Return to the Native Land*.

20 ***Bêtes-longues*** According to a belief of African origin, saying the name of a snake can cause it to appear, so 'the Long-beast' is used instead, and the most feared *bet-lonng* in Martinique is the deadly viper *Bothrops lanceolatus*, a fer-de-lance, the Unnameable. Père Labat wrote of a fer-de-lance nine feet long, but snakes that size are gone from Martinique, along with many other fauna and flora.

23 **marooning** The French *marron* is an abbreviation from the Spanish *cimarrón*, meaning *wild and unruly*, from *cima*, *mountaintop*. A Caribbean *mawonnè*, a *nègre marron*, was originally a fugitive black slave, a Maroon, and the term is now used for the descendants of such slaves. Africans imported during the Spanish period may have provided the first runaways in Jamaica, and some Maroons there still live in isolated, self-governing enclaves in the rugged hills.

31 **abolition** Slavery was finally completely abolished in French territory in 1848. By act of the British Parliament, the Abolition of the Slave Trade Act 1807 outlawed the slave trade in the British Empire, but

slavery itself was not abolished there until the Slavery Abolition Act 1833. In 1807, the U.S. Congress abolished the slave trade in the United States in the Act Prohibiting Importation of Slaves, a federal law that took effect in 1808. Although President Lincoln issued the Emancipation Proclamation in 1863, slavery in the United States did not end officially until the ratification of the Thirteenth Amendment to the Constitution, in 1865.

32   *basilic Basilic* means the culinary herb basil; the basilisk, a mythical reptile with a deadly breath or gaze, hatched by a snake from a rooster's egg; a mammoth cannon used in the sixteenth and seventeenth centuries; the green basilisk lizard of tropical American rain forests that can run on its hind legs across water. Your choice!

33   *hautes-tailles* Named for the high-waisted gowns of the time, the Martinican *haute-taille* is a quadrille that was popular in Europe and its colonies from the late 1700s through the 1800s and was adopted by slaves for their own amusement. The dance is for four couples in a rectangular formation and is related to American square dancing. And as Chamoiseau has pointed out, it is a 'dance during which the caller gives directions the dancers *must* follow.'

35   *chabines* Reflecting a mix of white and black genes, generally with light skin, eyes and hair, *chabin* men

and *chabine* women are sometimes stereotyped: they can be seen as 'all good or all bad' and have a reputation for willfulness and stubbornness. *Chabines* are thought to be impetuous and a bit mean.

38   **pepper sauce** A common punishment, even for things like stealing food, was whipping. Turpentine, hot pepper, salt pickle, lime juice, etc., were then rubbed into the wounds as antiseptics, but healing wounds were sometimes reopened to repeat the process as torture.

39   *sans manman* To be mama-less is the worst of fates, so as a general modifier, *sans manman* means merciless, unscrupulous, lowdown, dirty, etc., while a *sans-manman* person is a heartless scoundrel, scum, trash, an outlaw, or whatever else the context requires.

41   *Krik-Krak* A *kontè kréyol* – Creole storyteller – calls out 'Kri?' to announce the beginning of his set and demand the attention of his audience, who respond 'Kra!' to prove their vigilance in this ritual collaboration. Riddles, rhymes, proverbs, tales, wordplay of all kinds, inspired nonsense, 'multi-entendres,' animal noises, sound effects, expert drumming, etc., are accompanied by the *kontè*'s histrionics, subtle touches, and mimicry, which deliver an improvised performance completely focused on *animating the human voice* in communion with the faithful listeners, who join in as their spirits move.

48 ***chapeau-bakoua*** A *bakwa* is both the common screw
pine and a conical, wide-brimmed hat made of its
fronds that is so popular that when the Devil is in
Martinique, even he wears one.

51 **Marie Celat** In a sweeping series of novels, Édouard
Glissant traces the complicated relationships between
the descendants of two African men, one of whom
betrays the other to slavers, who in 1788 ship them
both on the *Rose-Marie* to Fort-de-France, where they
are sold to rival planters. Longoué soon escapes, while
Béluse remains in slavery. In *Le quatrième siècle* (*The
Fourth Century*), the *béké* planter La Roche, who has
hunted his slave Longoué for ten years, finally cedes
him some land, sealing the pact by tossing him a
piece of ebony bark into which the Maroon's likeness
has been incised, and a cask containing an accursed
Bête-longue and some gunpowder originally intended
to blow up Longoué. Passing from generation to generation, this cask becomes an increasingly mysterious
archive of Martinican history, as characters yearning
for a sustaining communal identity wonder what 'fer-
ment' really remains inside it, including, perhaps, 'the
color of their nightmares.'

In the end the cask passes from Papa Longoué, a
quimboiseur and guardian of his people's collective
memory, to Marie Celat (b. 1928), who in *La case
du commandeur* (*The Overseer's Cabin*) has a vision

one night of the 'unbearable absence of origin': 'She saw the bottom of a sea, the measureless blue of an ocean where lines of bodies attached to cannonballs descended dancing, and when she closed her eyes she descended with the drowned into that blue devoid of all escape.'

Captives died in huge numbers along the African slave routes in journeys that could take from weeks to even years, while many died during long incarcerations in coastal prisons, but the number of deaths during the Middle Passage alone is usually set at around two million. In *La case du commandeur*, a narrative voice observes that about fifty million are said to have been tossed into the ocean to sink – or wash ashore as sea-foam.

55 ***Ti-sapoti*** The 'Li'l sapotillas' are goblins who live in groups in trees and play mean jokes on people, whom they enjoy keeping awake at night with their shrieks and racket.

55 ***soucougnans*** *Soukliyans* remove their skins at night and hang them on a nail at home, then fly as balls of fire through the sky to the homes of their victims, slipping through cracks or keyholes to drink human blood, leaving behind telltale bruises. In a pinch, animal blood will do. Experts claim they are always women, for only a woman's breasts can change into wings.

55 ***coquemares*** Named after the French word for night-
    mare, *cauchemar*, these creatures attack sleeping
    people and are the relatively harmless spirits of babies
    who died unbaptized.

57 **nail barrel** Plantations made free use of the ever-
    popular torture (read 'The Goose Girl' in *Grimms'
    Fairy Tales*) of cramming a victim into a nail-studded
    barrel and rolling it down a hill.

63 **the Trace** As in the Natchez Trace, this North
    American and West Indian word refers to a beaten
    path or small road, which here was a track in
    Martinique first used by Jesuits in the seventeenth
    century to link Fort-de-France with Saint-Pierre.
    What is now the N3 crossed the rugged interior of the
    island, covered with tropical forest now showcased
    in the botanical park of Balata, and a section is still
    called the Route de la Trace. The Pont de l'Alma is
    a small bridge where the route out of Fort-de-France
    begins to climb to the wooded heights of Balata.

      In *Le discours antillais* (*Caribbean Discourse*),
    Glissant evokes the heady fragrances of his childhood,
    the smell of wild lilies along La Trace, but 'all those
    flowers have disappeared, or almost,' and the country
    seems to have 'renounced its essence' in favor of ster-
    ile appearance. And the Route de la Trace, of course,
    also embodies the difficult quest for the occulted past
    of the island.

67   **bon-ange** This 'good-angel' is the part of the soul that reflects someone's individual qualities, their personality, character, and willpower.

70   **three-hooves** It is rank bad luck to see the diabolical *chouval-twa-pat*, for this three-leg-horse pulled a hearse in life.

70   **silk-cotton trees** Spirits love to live in the ceiba pentandra, also called the giant kapok, a huge tropical deciduous tree much prized by *quimboiseurs* for its magical properties.

70   **Agiferrant** In *Culture et société aux Antilles françaises* (1972), Jean Benoist recorded this information from an uneducated old man: 'The Moon is a ball of water. A man named Agiferrant has lived there a long time. He refused to carry Christ's cross and was condemned to travel all over the Earth. One day, tired of being insulted, he took refuge on the moon. At least that's what my father told me.'

70   **treasure** Many Caribbean islands have stories about *béké* treasure buried at night in a hole that becomes the grave of the slave who dug it, who is thus bound to protect his master's riches until set free by a successful treasure hunter. Chamoiseau's *Chronicle of the Seven Sorrows* tells the tale of a market porter in Fort-de-France who in the end makes friends with Afoukal, a lonely zombie who rides his treasure jar up to the surface of the earth at night to chat with him.

When the porter goes gold-crazy and breaks open the jar, bones and jar crumble to clay and dust, and as he fades away, Afoukal sorrowfully tells his friend, now doomed to be eaten by a *djables*, that 'not all riches are gold: there is memory . . .'

70   **Ti-cochons-sianes** In May, nights can be noisy when a pack of these little pigs runs around and around a house yapping and squeaking. If the householder opens the door, the pigs vanish, but there stands a big strong man without head or arms.

70   **dream** Dreaming about pigeon peas means you'll soon find some money; dreaming of having a tooth extracted means a close relative will die; dreaming at midnight is a sign of death; dreams about bread warn of misfortune.

70   **Pamoisés** These people are so mean that they can turn into dogs, and their crooked thumbs give them away, because the nails look like dog claws.

71   **Dorlis** This creature is a succubus/incubus without any well-defined physical form and may take the shape of an animal or be invisible. The *Dorlis* forces itself sexually on sleeping men or women, and the only way to be safe is to leave some peas, beans, pebbles, grains of sand, etc. in a container or scattered on the floor, as the *Dorlis* will be compelled to count them and must leave by dawn.

71   **La Bête à Man Ibè** 'Madame Hubert's Beast' is this

witch's familiar, a maleficent animal, and Man Ibè is
known for her bloodcurdling screams.

74 *Fer Fè* means iron, and as an exclamation it encom-
passes the gamut of dramatic situations, serious
problems, and real suffering.

77 **trace back the names** In Glissant's 'La folie Celat'
(The Celat Madness), in *Le monde incréé*, Marie Celat
evokes the names of the dead:

'I have so many names in me.[...] I spoke the
names, right at that moment, what use is it?[...] I had
peered into the cask. Nothing but the cane-trash of
time.[...]

'After all these years we have been crossing, without seeing the trace, the time has come to unblock the
path, to trace back the names.'

The corrosive suffering of Marie Celat reflects
the sickness of Martinique itself and the need to
ground its people in time and place through the
reappropriation of their past and their presence on
the island.

'I am the rock. ... Behold my bones dry out in
my flesh gone to chalk. I appear and disappear, like
a thrown rock. Take me, throw me into your derail-
ing mass hysterias, throw me into your carnivals,
under your plague of traffic, into your Monoprix
chain stores, through the plate-glass window where
your simpering grimaces grin back at you.[...] What

is capsizing in my head?. ... Ah! What's spinning round? The names the names the names. ...'

It is when Marie Celat finally assumes the care of souls who alone know their lost names that she moves toward redemption, as if bearing away all sins: 'I have so many names in me. ... Never mind, I carry them away uncounted, so that my salvation may come.'

It is time to trace back the names: 'And it isn't that I want to fall into this night, either, but the night falls in me, with all the rain.'

79 **seventh wave** There is a folk belief that ocean waves travel in groups of seven, and that the last one is the biggest wave.

86 **three Ebony trees** Crossroads are the favorite haunt of spirits and demons, and a crossroads where three ebony trees shelter under a mahogany tree is a vital space in the Longoué and Béluse family saga novels of Glissant, for whom landscape is a character in both story and history. The scene of a murder, this crossroads is the scene of its own murder when corrupt 'progress' uproots the ebony trees (among which the ancestral Maroon had thrust his cutlass into the soil in a defiant gesture against La Roche), a living link with the past, leaving a wound that never heals: 'the lost trace found lost' (*Malemort*).

90 **Brittany** Crewed by dead or damned sailors and pirates, sometimes under the lash of giant dog demons

and so forth, ghost ships have long haunted the coast of Brittany and its Gulf of Morbihan. And it's never good luck to see one.

90   **cat bones** One West African tradition transplanted to the Caribbean and the American South was the use of black-cat bones, thought to give invisibility to their possessors, since black cats are hard to see at night.

97   **Carib** The indigenous inhabitants of the West Indies, who migrated from mainland America, were a complex collection of peoples including the Ciboney, the Taino-Arawak, and the Kalinago or Carib, whose migrations went through the chain of islands. Displacement was by peaceful assimilation or warfare, as in the raids by the fierce Carib that drove the Taino to the north in the 1400s.

98   ***pétun*** Tobacco was called *pétun* in a now-extinct Caribbean language.

98   ***cannamelle*** This is an old French word for sugarcane, *cane à miel*, 'honey-cane.'

98   **the volcano** Mount Pelée began its most famous eruptions on April 23, 1902. On May 8 it devastated Saint-Pierre, the largest city on the island, with lava and pyroclastic flows, killing about thirty thousand people. An equally violent eruption on May 20 destroyed what remained of the city, killing two thousand people who had arrived to help. On August 30, a pyroclastic flow reaching farther eastward killed

about a thousand people in those areas. The volcano is now semi-active.

100 **papaya and boredom** Born in Guadeloupe in 1887, Saint-Jean Perse was a French poet-diplomat who won the Nobel Prize in Literature, and within his cycle of West Indian poems, 'Pour fêter une enfance' ('To Celebrate a Childhood') describes remembered family and servants: 'And I did not know all Their voices, and I did not know all the women, all the men who served in the high wooden house; but for a long time yet my memory holds mute faces, the color of papaya and boredom, that stopped behind our chairs like dead stars.'

106 **hydromel** Hydromel is a mixture of water and honey that when fermented becomes mead, an alcoholic beverage.

113 ***Oriamé l'Africaine*** This *entre-dire* by Glissant deepens an opening into Chamoiseau's text already begun by Marie Celat. Oriamé was also on the slave ship *Rose-Marie*, where the female captives were at the mercy of the crew. In 'La folie Celat,' in *Le monde incréé*, Glissant speaks of Oriamé, the first in the long line of his women fated to resolute solitude:

'Oriamé rose in an ocher morning, already the rocks were tumbling down inside her.

'The ridge of acomas and redwoods, where night has laid a crazy coverlet, stretches out in the West. It is Africa, and it is not. The Before Land, where we do not know which mouth has gaped wide and closed again.[. . .]

'Oriamé sees the boat that will deport her into the unknown, and the railing from which she will throw herself into the waters, finally knowing the sea, the unknowable sea. She beholds in the distance Marie Celat.[. . .]

'Oriamé ... reappears in Mariséla, to go away again. She has borne that stone, which is a rock. Where has she put it down? And where then, where has she lost it, if not in the depths of the sea?'

113 **the great wind** In 'La folie Celat,' in *Le monde incréé*, Marie Celat evokes the blowing sands of time and submerged memory that drive her wanderings:

'Before, formerly, once upon a long time ... The country man ran beneath the cloud, went up went down with it, traced his body in the woods and ravines. They cry that he's crazy, but he recites the geography, he spells in the breeze. What does it bring us, all this wind? "All this wind," says papa Longoué. Seeds and sands emptying out from the land of Africa, without counting the little creatures set wandering as well over this ocean. And if you search through this same said ocean, then you discover how-many paths paced among the stars of the depths, where you count up the Africans secured with cannonballs, poured out in chains into the abyssal deep.'

Oriamé's stone of sorrow has grown larger in the sandy ocean depths. Marie Celat feels impelled to give voice in the night. 'La folie Celat' ends with a dialogue between Marie Celat, of the Longoué line, and Mathieu Béluse, whom she married in 1946. The text finishes in Beckettian fashion with Mathieu immobile, and Marie Celat 'gone without moving':

'I want to cry out.

'I want to give birth to the words in my throat, that you have – not one – understood. Seek deep into your-selves, there where everything is bristling, on edge, then you shudder at the very thing you do not under-stand.[...] I want to shout words into your crackling bonfires, words you hear without understanding, and you are blinded.'

(In *La case du commandeur*, Marie Celat is released from an asylum in 1978.)

117 **solibo** A *solibo* is a pratfall or a roll down a hill, and one carnival evening in Fort-de-France, the Creole storyteller Solibo Magnifique dies in Chamoiseau's novel of the same name, from an *égorgette de la parole*: his throat cut by a word.

117 **vermicelles-diable** The *vémicel-djab, Cuscuta ameri-cana*, is a parasitic vine with long orange tendrils (the 'vermicelli') that help it cover bushes and trees until it smothers them.

118 **Bêtes-à-diable** The firebug and the ladybug have

similar coloration, but the latter, named after Our Lady, is called the *bet-a-bondié* in Martini-can Creole, the Good-Lord bug, while the *bet-a-djab* gets the devil's name because it likes heat.

120   **Job's tears** *Coix lacryma-jobi* is a tall grass that produces the perfect bead: a beautifully polished seed with a hole through it.

124   *évohé* Evoe is the Latinized form of the ritual cry of the bacchantes, who invoked Dionysus during the ecstatic dancing at their bacchanals in honor of the god.

127   ***Territory*** Born on an island scarred by the results of violent *de*-territorialization and genocide, Glissant challenged the very concept of Territory after what he saw as the loss of everything that would justify or bless a people's presence there. In the era of globalization, of Terra, he championed diversity as the real origin of human communities throughout the world. Such forms of identity recognize themselves in *relation*, not opposition, to 'the other,' as exemplified in the composite cultures of creolization.

135   ***Marqueur de Paroles*** Glissant's 1988 preface to Chamoiseau's *Chronicle of the Seven Sorrows* referred to the author as the *Marqueur de Paroles*, the Word Scratcher, and this character first appeared in Chamoiseau's own work in *Solibo magnifique* as the writer who investigates the death of the champion

Creole storyteller Solibo. Wherever he appears in Chamoiseau's work, the Word Scratcher agonizes over the role of literature for a people whose culture is oral, whose 'oraliture' is waning, and who are foundering without memory and identity, so that he must try to give them a lifeline into literature with the scratching of his pen.

135 **Morne-Rouge** Named after its reddish volcanic soil, Morne Rouge is the highest town in Martinique and lies along the Trace. The large pyroclastic flow of August 30, 1902, buried Morne Rouge and killed hundreds of people in the last fatal eruption of Mount Pelée to date. The town is now the site of a yearly pilgrimage in honor of Notre-Dame de la Délivrance, the patron saint of the island, who had spared the town in answer to the inhabitants' prayers on May 8, when an earlier eruption devastated the city of Saint-Pierre.

136 **let their chains drift with the street** *Qui livrent leurs chaînes aux rues* comes from the Creole expression *ba lari chenn*, which means 'to give chains to the street' – to cast off chains and vagabond, stroll aimlessly. And although wandering may be a sign of dispossession, in the esthetics of Créolité it is a privileged state, the mode of absorbing poetic consciousness that blurs boundaries and opens the soul to *what is*.

136   **three-caterpillar absinthe** The medical usage of absinthe *wormwood* dates back to ancient Egypt, and the word *wormwood* refers to its traditional role as a vermifuge, to worm animals and people. Like the 'worm' in a tequila bottle, these caterpillars vouch for the potency of the alcohol.

136   **a work** This is Chamoiseau's footnote: *Texaco*, novel, Éditions Gallimard, Paris, 1992.

138   ***Kouli*** After slavery was abolished in Martinique in 1848, unskilled East Indian laborers were recruited to replace slaves who had abandoned the *béké* plantations. Later in the century there was a small influx of Chinese immigrants, who tended to take up shopkeeping, along with Syrian/Lebanese arrivals, who specialized in retailing cloth, clothes, and household goods.

145   **Oiseau de Cham** Most of Chamoiseau's noms de plume in his texts derive from *cham(p)*, 'field,' and *oiseau*, 'bird,' and include Zibié (from the French word *gibier*, 'game,' now used for any kind of bird), Chamzibié (field-bird), and Oiseau de Cham (Bird of Ham – the son of Noah long considered the ancestor of African peoples).

155   **beguine** The beguine is a dance and style of music that originated in Martinique and Guadeloupe in the nineteenth century, fusing contemporary *French* ballroom dance steps with *West Indian bélé* music strongly influenced by *African* rhythms.

ABOUT THE AUTHOR

Born in Martinique, **Patrick Chamoiseau** is the author of twelve novels, including *Solibo magnifique*, *Chronique des sept misères*, and *Texaco*, which won the Prix Goncourt, was named a *New York Times* Notable Book of the Year, and has been translated into fourteen languages. He is one of the founding theoreticians of the Créolité movement.

ABOUT THE TRANSLATOR

Linda Coverdale has a PhD in French Studies and has translated more than eighty books. A Chevalier de l'Ordre des Arts et des Lettres, she has won the 2004 International IMPAC Dublin Literary Award, the 2006 Scott Moncrieff Prize, and the 1997 and 2008 French-American Foundation Translation Prize.

Bringing a book from manuscript to what you are reading is a team effort.

Dialogue Books would like to thank everyone at Little, Brown who helped to publish *The Old Slave and the Mastiff* in the UK.

Editorial
Sharmaine Lovegrove
Jennie Rothwell
Dom Wakeford
Simon Osunsade

Contracts
Megan Phillips

Sales
Sara Talbot
Ben Green
Barbara Ronan
Rachael Hum
Viki Cheung

Design
Helen Bergh
Nico Taylor

Production
Nick Ross
Narges Nojoumi

Publicity
Ella Bowman

Marketing
Jonny Keyworth
Kimberley Nyamhondera

Proofreader
Susi Elmer

Also from Dialogue Books

Who is a roadman really? What's wrong with calling someone a 'lighty'? Why do people think black guys are cool?

These are just some of the questions being wrestled with in *Black, Listed*, an exploration of 21st century black identity told through a list of insults, insights and everything in-between.

Part historical study, part autobiographical musing, part pop culture vivisection, it's a comprehensive attempt to make sense of blackness from the vantage point of the hilarious and insightful psyche of Jeffrey Boakye.

It is 1910 and Philadelphia is burning.

The last place Spring wants to be is in the rundown, coloured section of a hospital surrounded by the groans of sick people and the ghost of her dead sister. But as her son Edward lies dying, she has no other choice.

All Spring knows is that time is running out. She has to tell him the story of how he came to be. With the help of her dead sister, newspaper clippings and reconstructed memories, she must find a way to get through to him. To shatter the silences that her governed her life, she will do everything she can to lead him home.